Janice Shinebourne

Timepiece

Peepal Tree Press

Peepal Tree Press
53, Grove Farm Crescent
Leeds LS16 6BZ
Yorkshire
England

ISBN 0 948833 03 3

To B, Ty, Roddy, Rick and Mac

...for the growing good of the world is partly dependent on unhistoric acts; and that things are not so ill
with you and me as they might have been, is half
owing to the number who lived faithfully a hidden
life, and rest in unvisited tombs.

George Eliot *Middlemarch*

Prelude

The woman who got off the bus was a stranger. She was dressed in a blue blouse and trousers. When the blue wooden bus manoeuvred into turning round, and drove back in the direction it had come from, she waited at the roadside, watching him.

The cigarette burnt down to his fingers. He threw it under the culvert, into the drain. What did she want?

"Morning," she called out.

She meant only to walk around, look, and then leave when the bus returned. The villages in Canefields were not as she remembered them. During the drive from New Amsterdam, only two or three weather-beaten houses broke the monotony of bush. But when she saw him sitting on the culvert, smoking a cigarette, it was a vivid signal to her memory. He was, immediately, all the young boys of Pheasant who used to lounge round the culverts smoking and talking.

His trousers were rolled up to his knees. His T-shirt was threadbare. From the culvert, the path led back between the bush and overgrowth, to the canefields etched agelessly against the horizon.

She picked up her bag and walked towards him. He rose and assumed a relaxed stance, folding his arms. The strong breeze blew her hair clean back.

"I used to live here," she said.

He frowned. "I live here," he said.

She turned and pointed to the dying house across the road. "There," she said.

She had glimpsed it when the bus stopped and did not dare to look. She picked up her bag and crossed the road.

The gates were broken off their hinges and collapsed among the vines of the overgrowth. The concrete path which used to lead to the shop was shattered into chunks and half buried in the earth. The house she had lived in was there before her eyes, in decay. She walked up the broken path, through the gap where the gates used to be and was confronted with the final proof of its absolute decay. The supporting frame was naked here, on this side of the house. Loose planks hung like broken ribs from the frame and there were shapeless spaces where once there were doors and windows.

The boy had followed her. He assumed the same relaxed stance and watched her with open curiosity now.

"Where you from?" he asked her.

"Georgetown," she replied. "I travel down this morning and staying in New Amsterdam. I was abroad, and only lately come back."

She walked past him, out of the yard, and crossed the road. She sat on one wall of the culvert and he sat on the opposite wall.

"Noor, Zena, Miss Barry, Mitch, Miss K, Nurse Nathaniel - you know these people?" she asked him.

He thought briefly. "Nathaniel yes. I know a Nathaniel. Me friend. He living in New Amsterdam. But I don' know these other people you call. I don' know if is the same Nathaniel."

"What Nathaniel he is?"

"Dennis."

She shrugged. She stamped her feet and loosened the straps of her sandals. "God! This heat!" she exclaimed.

"Away cold, eh?"

"Bad."

"But the education good?"

She laughed, for she remembered what T had said about education many years ago. "You want education?" she asked him.

"Yes," he replied. "I going to the technical college in Georgetown - me and me friend Nathaniel. We come home every weekend but during the week, we board and lodge in Georgetown."

"I used to know a fellow called T here. He had a farm up in the forest. You know a fellow call T?"

He shook his head. "I don' know anybody call T. The forest dead. Not one man jack living there. Creek water flood 'way

6

everything. Pure bush there now - worse than here. I know once upon a time people use to live there but not now. People lef' here plenty. Only one two people living he' now."

"What about the estate?"

He shook his head again. "Estate work dead. Estate don' pay no kinda money. Estate only employing a few people nowadays. Pure machinery doing everything. Me old lady tell me long ago was pure estate work round he'. But not now."

She could feel the heat on her head now, burning through her hair. "T used to farm," she repeated herself. "He used to have a lotta boats. I used to go up there a lot."

"Me daddy might know him."

"What your daddy name?"

"Chuck. You know him?"

"No. You sure you don't know any of the people I asking you about?"

"No. But one two people he' might know though. You want ask?"

She looked round and shook her head. "No. Pure bush. Long ago this place was spick and span, with plenty houses, plenty people."

"My old lady say estate used to weed and clean the place."

"They were supposed to. They were supposed to do a lotta things they didn't do, like the weeding and cleaning, like providing medical services for workers, oh it was terrible. It was thanks to the people themselves the place was spick and span." She paused. "Must be five, six hundred people used to live here."

"Must be 'bout twenty people living here now."

"I don't think anybody would know Noor or Zena, or Nurse, Miss K or Miss Barry. They must be done dead and gone."

He sighed. "Man, you come till he' to look fo' ole time people an' expec' to find them?"

"Noor and Zena used to live in this same street. They didn't have children. But everybody else in this street had mus' be seven, eight children. Noor was a nice woman, a solid strong sorta woman in a sensible, warm sorta way. One time I t'ief from

7

her fruit trees. She catch me, wring me ears then hand me a basket and tell me to pick and eat till me belly full. All the women used to come and tell her their worries. Zena was another story. Zena husband never home. He had a woman in Jubilee had children fo' him. It used to drive poor Zena crazy and she used to take one or two shots a' rum to calm herself down. She used to send me to buy her rum and my old lady fell out with her over it. Zena mouth was hot! If you didn't answer her back she would take her eyes and pass you. She and Noor were best a' friends."

He was watching her intently, and listening, waiting for her to go on. But she said nothing else, only glanced once at the house across the road.

He said, "I like to hear ole time story. My ole people don' remember much. But they might know these people you talkin' about. You might even know them. You want come and meet them?"

We might be strangers she thought; they might have forgotten her and she them. It might be an empty ritual. How old was he? Seventeen? Such a difference between them - not just of years.

"What's your name?" she asked him.

"Mark."

"Where your parents live?"

He pointed to the path which led behind the house. "Behind there. People live at the back."

He began to walk along the path. She followed him. Just bush along here too. She used to feel that the forest would reach out and claim all the villages in Canefields, the way things were, with life so precarious and dependent on the estate. It was probably doing just that now.

Just one cottage at the end of the path. The canal was there too; its brown body glistened in the sunlight. She used to swim there. She resisted the urge to turn back.

A couple were sitting on the front steps. The woman was plump, her hair tightly curly like Mark's but thinner and longer, worn loose over her shoulders. When she saw them approach, a

8

look of shyness, like a veil, came over her face. The man, unperturbed, watched them. He wore only a pair of khaki trousers, and sat on the landing, a white enamel cup in his right hand.

Mark spoke to them. "Look, a lady come to visit." He was standing with her on the little wooden bridge which joined the path to the steps.

Now they all watched her and waited for her to speak.

She turned, walked to the path, stooped and vomited into the grass. She felt a touch on her shoulder. Mark's mother had brought her water in a white enamel cup and a faded towel. She took them, saying, "Thank you." She washed her face and mouth then dried herself with the towel. Mark's mother reached out to take the cup and towel.

"Mark, where you' visitor come from?" his father was asking.

She did not hear Mark's quiet reply.

"Nothing here to see," Mark's mother said.

She spoke to Mark's mother, "I come because I used to live here."

"Where?" she asked.

She pointed back along the path. "The old house by the road."

"Oh...yes...." Her face cleared slowly.

"Long time..."

Mark's mother gestured with her hand for her to be silent. She pressed the tips of her fingers into her cheek and looked down at the ground, as if the key to her memory were written there in words which only she could decipher. Then she spoke, "Yes, my mother use to tell me ole time story but I was young then. I remember she telling me 'bout a family use to live in de' ole house. She say cinema use to work here them days and it make the place lively bad. But you know, de estate shuttin' down make this place go dead. People move 'way so nobody lef' to remember. An' when de estate start up again a different set a people work on it."

Mark and his father came to the gate.

"You o.k. now?" Mark's father asked.

9

"Yes."

"Why you vomit so, man?" He was concerned. "You hungry?"

"No thank you."

"You sure?"

"Yes, sure."

"Mark tell me you come from away."

"Yes. I travel from Georgetown this morning."

"Why you come till he'?"

"I come to see the place."

"Man, nothing in he' to see. You can' see is pure bush he' an we one two people?"

Mark's mother turned to her husband. "She used to live he'. In de ole house. I tell she I remember my mother use to talk about a family use to live de'. But I can' remember much." She paused. "If people di'n go away so much I would remember everything. If people di'n go away you would have bound to meet all de people you lookin' for. Me and me husband and we one two neighbours only living he'. Me husband work in New Amsterdam."

"Ye' man," her husband said, "things change up bad he'. I don' belong here you know. I married and come to live he' by my wife had this house, by her daddy wanted to leave Pheasant an' go work with the bauxite company, an' I find work easy in New Amsterdam. We neighbours don' belong he'. Only my wife belong he'. I work in New Amsterdam. I drive trucks."

Mark walked back to the road with her.

The bus used to go all the way to the forest, but now it turned back here, in Pheasant. It arrived in a cloud of dust.

"Thanks, Mark," she said, as she got on the bus.

He nodded. "All the best then."

"And to you too," she returned.

Pheasant as she had known it was dead. All the fuss and fury of its life had ceased. What was here now was an unperturbed presence. Where cottages once stood, the bush had grown back. The buildings that remained were a reminder of the life before

10

only to those who had known it. The estate was not interested in Pheasant because it no longer drew labour from it. The bush was claiming Pheasant. Pheasant was at its own ease. Unperturbed, Mark and his parents continued to live there. To them, its memories and history were ineffectual, to Mark because he was taken up with his education in Georgetown, to his mother because she could not remember it, because her memories had vanished. They had not taken up where others had left off. They were like first people here. The slate of their memory was clean.

I

In the days following the end of school, Sandra would wake early, as her grandmother Sarah used to do, and go to the window to watch the dawn break. Sarah had sat at the window, with the view before her.

The upper half of the view was pure sky, the lower half contained the village: rows of cottages on either side of the parallel paths which ran adjacent to the horizontal road. The horizon cut across the two halves of the landscape, itself divided by two thick lines: one the green canefields in the distance, the other the brown canal beside it.

Sarah had not liked being useless. Her fruit and grain stall at Stabroek Market in Georgetown was gone; her home in La Penitence there one day, gone the next. She was used to independence; dependence vexed her. Only the peace at dawn calmed her. She had come to live with them to escape the racial disturbances which began in Georgetown in 1961, spread to many other parts of the country and did not end until 1964, by which time fifteen thousand people, mostly Indo-Guyanese, had been forced to move their homes and settle elsewhere. It seemed as if for many people these disturbances occurred long ago. They talked of the independence to come in a year or so. It was happening too fast: no time to mourn, no time to grieve. It was the same with Sarah. She died soon after she came to stay, with only time enough for her to plant up the vegetable garden.

When Sarah died, Sandra took her room. It was the best room, a modern extension, with the guinep tree growing against one wall, and the mango tree near the other. Their branches grew and met, hugging the house. Through the open shutters the light would clear the distance, wash the sky lightly at first, then break through the clouds and arrive to soften the room. In time, the sun rose, a ball of light, and cast the village in its everyday, familiar mould.

Some two hundred yards north-east of Pheasant, the overseers lived in white bungalows. Opposite the bungalows lay the sprawling sugar factory: a huge complex of high and low level steel and concrete buildings, with several tall chimneys rising from the zinc roofs. Further south, where the road narrowed to a grassy track, was the forest, a twisted mass of huge tree trunks, thick vines and dense foliage, penetrable only by travelling along the waterway. People lived on the frontal outskirts of the forest, in the clearings and on the savannahs, where they kept small farms.

The hint of light in the East grew, the sky gave way to it, the clouds shifted. Grey shapes, shadows and textures altered into the familiar colours: greens on the land, the flaming colours of the flowers, ethereal and shapeless among the greens; all still overhung with the fading mist.

In the half-light, there seemed hardly any distance between the sky and the land, between a floating mass of cloud and a rooftop. It was as if the land were shifting upwards, the sky lowering itself, so they would meet and the one pass through the other, like invisible things.

The house was asleep, Helen and Ben in their bedroom, Jay and William in the middle bedroom. Helen's sewing machine was open and threaded. Her sewing things were spread out on the table. The book which Jay had been reading lay open. Ben's Berbice chair was as he had left it the night before, with the arms pushed out to form a footrest. The village slept too.

The canefields always seemed undisturbed in the distance, but in the daytime people were there in their numbers, working in the heat. After daybreak, the red lorries, loaded with men and women, passed up and down along the road, taking and bringing the labourers to and from the canefields.

Five years ago, those lorries took away some of her poorest schoolfriends, Ralph Brijlall, Unis Ali, Joe Tiwari, to the canefields. Ralph went to cut cane, Unis to bale punts and Joe to catch rats in the canefields. The poorest girls left school earlier to help mind their family and do housework or to work the small farms in the savannah, or at the saw mill or become servants,

13

some even making their way to work for white overseers eventually. The girls who survived beyond Third Standard were Bibi Ali, Madeline Benjamin and Leila Mohammed. Madeline and Bibi were still auxiliary nurses at New Amsterdam Hospital and Leila helped at the Dispensary. The children whose parents were willing to struggle and send them to high school had sat secondary school entrance examinations. Few passed them; Sandra had been the only girl in Pheasant that year to pass. Several girls from the third village on, Good Land, also passed - the daughters of shopkeepers, the owner of the cinema and the daughters of the bus driver - people who did not depend on the sugar plantation for a living. But they had chosen to go not to Berbice High School but to the new non-denominational school on the other side of New Amsterdam. Families in two minds about Christianity, like her own, or converted to Christianity sent their children to Berbice High School.

Five years had been a long time to cycle to and from New Amsterdam morning and afternoon, and sometimes at midday, which made it four journeys a day, totalling twelve miles. Those years took her even further away from her old schoolfriends. Working in the sun had toughened up Ralph, Unis and Joe overnight it had seemed. It parched their skin and turned their faces mean and weary - Unis now drank and gambled heavily and Joe was sickly. Ralph did not stay long on the estate. He was now living near the forest where he helped work a small farm there. Sometimes he brought them a sack of rice.

This year, more children than ever would begin high school. Those who had passed their exams were treated with ritual advice:

"Further yourself, my dear," Nurse Nathaniel said. "Live a good life, get more education if you can, my dear. Praise the Lord, my dear."

And Miss K: "Trust no man, whether he be your husband or whosoever. Man is no good."

And Zena: "Marry and make plenty children. Take care of your husband."

And Noor: "Be happy, Beti."

Each advice was different and spoke to her more of their

14

natures than gave her a single direction to follow.

Helen wanted her to go to Georgetown. Ben was against it. They disagreed about her future on principle. But the key to life did not lie in their hands but hers. Neither the education she received at school nor their advice would provide answers. Only a faith and belief that common truths lay behind their actions would guide her. People acted from the secrets of their nature; like the light and darkness, like the trees, the water and the land. Their natures were shaped by the varied conflicting currents which flowed within them. All these needed to be understood. Their restlessness provided the evidence, as they were tossed and turned, from town to village, home to factory, canefields, schools.

Whether or not she should leave Pheasant: this was not the issue. The issue was the vagueness of their intentions. She should 'better' and 'further' herself; marry, preferably a stranger, someone not from Pheasant; she should not be like them. The values which they hinted at were vague; they were large and ambitious, yet small and humble, double-edged with the benign tyranny of their ruthless good intentions. They were passing on a sense only of the future. But their own ordered life was composed of an indefinite past linked through memory to a present divided between their inner richness and their material poverty. Struggle linked positively all their experiences. And though they understood the present better than the past, and experienced it as more whole, they could guess that the past must have contained their own normal capacity for endurance and laughter. They were confident these qualities passed through their ancestors to them. Their confidence helped their laughter, contradictions and paradoxes to ring more deeply. For them, the future was helpless and blind, it could only lead beyond them, as it had done for people like themselves before their time, people from whom they extended as their own children extended from them. Yet it was to the future alone they were directing her.

Everyone and everything fitted into a niche here. Long before she was born, the canefields grew, were cut down, burnt, fed into the factory and the sugar sold. Where did people go if not to their graves? To the city, the town, the interior or other villages? Wherever they went, this order remained.

People would awake soon. They would have no time to watch morning break and wonder about these things. Predictable though the day was, it brought frustrations which claimed a person's mind and emotions. Even Sarah, with all the wisdom of her years, had been at seventy continually a victim. Her years of independence ended with two years of dependence. Each day of those two years had cheated her of pride, authority and discipline. She had enforced these on her poverty, to bring a pattern to her everyday activity which allowed her to rise from her bed and know the precise direction she would take. Those last two years deprived her of purpose and imagination.

The house was not depressed when Sarah died. Her presence was in the room long after. She was in the butterfly and the bird which landed in the room once. According to Laila, a butterfly or bird which visited after death was the spirit of the dead person returned. Was Sarah's spirit as quivering in its stillness as the brown butterfly's? Did her life, and those of the men and women she knew at Stabroek Market, really throb like the bird's? Sandra felt that if she touched them, she would touch Sarah's life; but she feared that if she moved towards the bird or butterfly, if she got close, if she tried to hold their life, her hands would be scorched. Yet she also knew that one burst from Jay's airgun would bring them down.

The women in this family, Sarah's daughters, were beautiful and rare like the bird and butterfly visiting the rooms of the living with nature's energy for life; beauty and energy which attracted violence easily. Sandra had visited Stabroek Market with Sarah. People there said: "You are Sarah's grandaughter, one of the Lau women." Some said it with a jealous look which Sarah met without fear. This exchange of feeling showed her where Sarah's strength came from, a strength which Sandra never doubted that Sarah and her daughters possessed. That was until the events in Wismar in 1963. They said that at Wismar women had held down women to be raped - Afro-

16

Guianese women held down Indo-Guianese women to be raped in revenge for their men preferring them, revenge against their men too. Violence was always a weapon used by one sex against the other sex, so it was inevitable it would be used by one race against the other.

When Sarah died, life had left her slowly. Ben, Helen, Jay and William were out. They were alone. Sarah knew when her time came and took her hand. Sandra had thought she was asleep, like a baby. The room was quiet as it was now, as softly shed with light, as informed with life: both theirs, the muffled noises of the village and the trees outside, whispering with the breeze.

Helen had wept; she and Sarah had quarrelled that afternoon. At night, the women's faces, Sarah's daughters and her friends, were flecked with the pale brass lamplight that was cast around the dark room like the light from a cloudbanked sunset. They sat in a circle round her bed. The daylight was miles away where they had come from: Essequibo, West Coast, East Coast. Helen's weeping was lonely in the room, like a note tapped our over and over on Pat's piano. The sudden appearance of Sarah's daughters and old friends brought home how distance and silence between people could be as expansive as the interior, until a telegram or message at midnight returned them to the insistent clearings, to form an old circle, letting the silence bind them together, while an ancient lamp was lit and watch kept over a corpse.

Sarah had taken her to Georgetown once, when she went for a day to revisit her old haunts. It was an early morning journey. Everyone was asleep. They sat together, a woman and a girl alone, at the misty roadside with their suitcases and heard the bus come from the forest: a deep rumbling within the ground. Everything emerged from the painted mist: a canecutter in grey rags, a red lorry in the orange-tinted light and, when nothing, the swirling vortex of dust. Even the light grew a shape in the dust, seeming to lower itself, like a silent being alighting to bless them. It was exciting to be alone, sitting on their traps, going to Georgetown. Even the rickety bus was silent. From the rear window of the bus Pheasant stretched away. Distance was elastic. Parts of her could rebound, be thrown back. Georgetown was yet miles away, a memory of noises. The further they drifted from Pheasant, the further the horizon receded; only fantasy lay beyond it.

When she let herself absorb the sadness of adults, it claimed her mind entirely. When school closed, she thought it would bring rest. Instead, awareness, like the leaves of a book, turned over and brought new facts to light.

Helen found her leaning on the sill, half-asleep.

Helen shook her, saying, "Wake up." It irritated her to see her idle.

"I fell asleep."

"You shouldn't get up so early in the morning. Go, bring water."

When she opened the back doors, the light filled the corridor. Miss Barry was bathing Nathan and Dorothy at the pipe in their yard. She emptied bowls of water over them. The children sulked.

Morning Miss Barry," she called out. " Why Nathan and Dorothy so grumpy?"

"Morning," Miss Barry returned. "They don' want to go to school, that's why. Tell them what would happen to them if they don't go to school!"

She sat the bucket under the water barrel and leaned over the fence. "Well, the school inspector will come looking for them."

Miss Barry emptied the last bucket of water over the children. "I din' mean that. I mean worse. They will end up cutting cane in the backdam, or doing servant work."

The men and women went by on their way to the estate. Each carried a saucepan of food and a cutlass. The overseers would allot them work. The unlucky ones would return home.

The paths between the cottages were narrow. Few were fenced. The wooden windows and doors had to be opened wide to let the light in, so there was little privacy. As you walked along the paths, the noises from the people's cottages, the people's voices and the clattering of pans in the kitchen were audible behind the rows of foliage in the flower and kitchen gardens, the only screens in most of the open yards.

She was using up her remaining time with work in the garden, helping Helen and Laila, and visiting Pat and T. The last five years had taken her away from the village. Now, she lost herself in the daily chores and talk. But when she was with Pat and T, and talk turned to the future, it was not easy to be casual. They reminded her she was leaving and speculated about her future.

She took the buckets upstairs. Jay was up. He stood in the doorway, arms akimbo, blocking her way.

"Tha's my bucket water," he bullied.

She ignored him, and squeezed past. He shoved her back. The water splashed their feet. Her temper flared, and she emptied the bucket over him. In a fury he seized her and they began to struggle. She was soon sitting on him, pinning his arms behind his back.

Helen came to the corridor. "Leave him!" she ordered.

When Jay was free, he flew at Helen and flayed her with his fists. She held his arms, and shook him. "Look you!"

He tore himself from Helen's grasp and ran to his room, Helen crying after him, "When you want to play big man, find y'u own house to play big man in!" William began taunting him. "You leave your big brother alone!" she ordered William. The room went quiet.

Ben appeared on the inner stairs. "Wha's this commotion?" he demanded. "Water dripping downstairs."

Helen pointed to her. "I don't know what to say to her. She so big and fighting with Jay."

"I not his slave," she retorted. "He try to take my water!"

Ben and Helen exchanged weary looks.

"Look," Ben said. "Try don' fight with y'u brothers. You too big for that sorta thing now. Try find things to do."

19

Helen turned to Ben. "What to do about Jay? That boy passion uncontrollable. You have to try to discipline him." She turned to Sandra. "Look, I too old for these things. Try and behave yourself."

There was no point in arguing with them. Bottling up her irritation, she went outdoors again. Helen was always pointing out the fact that they were getting old, and she becoming an adult. Now she had left school, they expected her to look after herself, fast.

She spent the next hour working in the garden. The guavas were splayed out like gay bulbs on the branches, and the peppers were withering from want of picking.

Laila came to the kitchen door when she arrived. She teased, "Eh girl, you pickin' guava fo' me?"

"Yes, for you to cook!"

Laila scowled. "My job in' to cook no guava!"

By the time she went in, Jay and William were gone to school. Ben and Helen were busy in the shop. Laila had put the pots on the fire: one filled with fresh milk which she brought every morning from her father's farm, the other filled with water. She was washing at the aluminium sink. Her bare arms were covered with white suds and the kitchen smelt richly of the salty soap. Laila began to sing an American pop song, 'Young Love'.

Laila was always singing. She sang Indian songs, calypsoes and British and American pop songs, mixing the incantations of the Indian songs, the rhythm of the calypsoes and the monotonous melodies of the pop songs.

When Laila went outside to wash the clothes, Sandra followed her, sitting on the steps to cut up the guavas. Laila talked about making guava jelly; how sweet or sour guavas could be, but if mixed in the right balance, such and such a flavour could be produced. She knew the flavours of all the guavas on all the neighbours' trees. She was in the middle of a sentence when she stopped, and beckoned to Sandra to turn around.

Josephine Marks was standing in the doorway.

"Josephine!"

20

They had not seen each other since school ended. Josephine was pleased at the surprise she had given her.

Josephine said, "I come to see you country folks in all your splendour." She pointed to Sandra's dress. "Look at you, all your clothes wet. What you doing?"

"Laila, you see what happen when town come to country?"

Josephine laughed. "Come inside, we can't sit on the steps and talk."

"Yes, Boss," Sandra joked.

"What you doing with those guavas? Making guava jelly?"

"Yes."

"You don't want to go to all that trouble. You can buy it in a bottle."

They sat at the table. Josephine was wearing a stiff, starched and ironed white blouse and blue jeans. She spun a bunch of keys round and round her left forefinger.

"You came by car?" Sandra asked Josephine.

"Yes. You all roads bad, man."

"Use the bus next time. These roads not made for cadillacs."

Josephine's parents owned two American cadillacs. They often drove her to school; that was the only time you saw Josephine's parents, behind the wheel of the two large cars. Once or twice, Josephine had driven to school herself.

Now Laila was in the kitchen. She had not finished the washing, but was taking the pots and pans from the cupboard. It was too early to begin cooking lunch; she was in there to eavesdrop.

Helen appeared with a tray of drink and cakes.

"Oh thank you, Mrs. Yansen," Josephine said brightly, enjoying the fuss.

"How Mummy and Daddy?" Helen asked.

"Oh fine, thank you," Josephine replied, sipping her drink.

"Sandra tell me you got eight 'O' levels."

21

"Yes," Josephine confirmed.

"Sandra only got seven, and no Maths. I hear you got Maths."

Laila was stifling her giggles. Helen gave her a cutting look.

"Yes," Josephine agreed.

Helen turned to go. "Well, I must go . Shop busy." She hesitated. "Sandra, so you treating your guest? Take Josephine upstairs."

She contradicted Helen, "Josephine all right down here."

When Helen was out of earshot, Josephine spoke, "You heard your old lady, take me up."

"Why? We can talk right here."

Josephine glared at Laila, "I don't like people listening to my conversations."

Laila flounced her skirt and declared huffily, "I in' listenin' to you conversation!"

"You don't teach her manners?" Josephine demanded to know.

"You better mind your mouth. Laila don't like people to tell her anything. Her mouth hot like pepper."

"Take me upstairs!" Josephine hissed.

As they climbed the stairs, Josephine complained, "I can't stand it when servants don't have manners. She look like one wild woman. What happen? You all short of real maids round here?"

"You tell Laila she's a maid, and she'll kill you."

"It seems to me you all give her far too much licence."

"Look Josephine, stop fretting. You'll get old before y'u time."

They sat in the morris chairs. Josephine commented on the strong breeze coming throught the open windows, the paraffin lamp which hung from the ceiling, and the bare zinc roof.

"You finish finding fault?" she asked Josephine.

"I not finding fault," Josephine replied, "I just never been in a country house before."

"Well now you see. You want to leave?"

22

Josephine rose and went to the window. She looked outside, spinning her keys, restless.

Josephine's restlessness stirred Sandra's own. They were out of school uniform, and killing time. Boredom brought her here; but whether or not she went away, Josephine would be all right. For herself, there was Georgetown, challenging her ignorance and threatening her security. Josephine could be a mystery, she had no friends, only people she went to when she felt like a chat. Mrs. Marks thought no one good enough for their family. Mrs. Marks had studied hairdressing in London and the schoolgirls were malicious about this, saying that Mrs. Marks behaved as if it were medicine and not hairdressing she had done, and that she had returned with a permanent chip on her shoulder and took it out on everyone. Josephine had adopted the burden of all her mother's ways, but she didn't see it. When you felt sympathy for Josephine she took advantage. Her look was precociously harsh and aggressive; she was quick tempered; she bore a deep resentment of country girls, and if they were bright, hated them for their very existence. At school, others had said that Josephine was dangerous, but Sandra disagreed; Josephine needed safety nets, people who could soothe her fears. She was small, thin, unathletic. On the fields, at games, the bigger girls got their own back. Josephine often retreated battered and bruised. Next day, Mrs. Marks would storm into the school to file a complaint. Josephine bullied in her own way; she forced her attitudes on others, with an intensity which was painful. There were lines round her mouth and a frown lay always at the ready on her forehead. Though she was rich, she carried injustice and injury about her person. The school's competitiveness, stresses and battles were here with Josephine. Now she was pacing up and down the room.

"Josephine, sit down," she pleaded. "You will wear yourself out."

"I have a lot of life in me yet, I will show them."

"Who upset you now?"

She pointed north in the direction of the town. "My old man. You know I ask him to pay my university fees, and he told me no?" She took pause enough to deepen her look of injured innocence. "He takes me for a fool. Who you think does his accounts? Me! He knows I know he has money! Is insult he want to insult me!" Now she looked angry and began to pace up and down again. "You wait," she raged, "one of these good days I will show them that no one can push me around, one of these good days."

"Well, how will you prevent that? Join the police force?"

"You hear how you laughing at me too?"

"Josephine," she pleaded. "Sit down! Relax! You too young!"

"Young? You realise we going into our twenties? You sit down here peeling guavas and talking to servants..."

"Josephine, if you say one more word about that..."

She sat down and sighed. "Anyway, what you intend to do?"

"I got a job in Georgetown."

"What job?"

"Trainee reporter, with the *Daily Mail*."

"Reporter?" Josephine was incredulous. "How far that will take you?"

She shrugged. "Who say I want it to take me far?"

"Lord! You make an art of being unambitious! What happen? What you frighten?"

"Who say I frighten anything?"

"Well, I suppose I should say congratulations. The only reporters I know always seem to be starving."

"The pay sounds good enough."

"Yes, for the time being. You need a lotta money in this world."

"What for?"

Josephine burst out laughing, then stopped abruptly. "I wish you luck."

"Well, thank you, you make it sound as if I going out to the wars, never to return."

"What about Pat?"

"Pat's alright."

"The two of you like Suru and Duru. Breeze don't pass through you two. She don' live far from here. You see each other a lot?"

Sandra nodded. Pat and Josephine disliked each other. Theirs was one of the famous 'hate relationships' at school.

"She found a job too?"

"Pat not looking yet."

"I suppose she has too much worries."

She stared at Josephine in alarm. "What worries? You know something I don't?"

Josephine smirked, and adopted her cat-who-swallowed-the-rat look. It hid something bad. Moments like these made Sandra certain that Josephine disliked her. She knew that if she questioned her closely, Josephine would take her time letting out her secret, prolonging the agony. She pretended not to care.

Josephine decided to break her silence. "Ah, that Edwards family is a joke."

Sandra rose. "Look, I have work to do."

"Her parents getting a divorce," Josephine announced.

"How you know that?"

"My parents know the lawyers in town, man. One of them told Mummy." Josephine was smiling.

"And that funny?"

"I didn't say that's funny. But what's funny is the way you like to pretend that nothing's wrong, Sandra Yansen. Everyone knows Pat's father has plenty outside women, and how Mrs. Edwards goes looking for them in all the offices to 'buse them down in public..."

"Josephine," she interrupted her. "You come all this way to tell me this?"

Josephine got up, "I going back to civilisation," she declared, and walked to the front door. She said, "See you," and left.

Five years ago when she started school in New Amsterdam it was all such a drama - the shock of it - going from a rural primary school where the majority of children went no further in their education but began to drop off after their fourth year. At high school in New Amsterdam she found a different world where the idea of lacking education was unthinkable, the alternative barbaric. Only the future mattered, a future where the lawyers, doctors, dentists and wealthy commercial class lived in large houses, with American cars and holidays in Europe and North America. The present and the past were to be put behind one, fast, as Josephine was doing, rushing to meet her future. School was already in the past, to be forgotten like all their past, sleep from which to wake.

In Pheasant, the sense of the past and future was different. Here, you could not forget the past, could not escape from it. It was not a fiction or fantasy. The canefields, the factory, the English overseers, were very real, so were the Amerindians and the freed slaves who still lived in the forest, still afraid of being recruited into plantation labour. Miss K and Noor were very real too; you could only think of Miss K as an African woman, you could only think of Noor as an Indian woman: two of the strongest women in Pheasant. In New Amsterdam they would not be taken seriously; they were too close to the past, to India and Africa where labour came from, to the sugar plantations where labour went to, and to the forest where the ex-slaves and Amerindians still lived. But because the past was so real in Pheasant, the future could only be entirely a fantasy. The motor cars and American films which came to the area had a magical appeal more powerful than visiting magicians, and so you had to entirely invent the future before you could go forward to meet it. Not so in New Amsterdam. The future was closer there, although still a little magical. It was there in Josephine and her kind including all the families untouched by the past, who could not bear to be touched by the past. They embraced the comforts of the future, never mind it was a transplanted one which they could only mimic, able to turn into fact only periodically when they went abroad to the U.S.A. for their holidays. At school they were prepared to take possession of the future, so that the world which raged outside, the present of race riots, local political intrigue and power struggles were viewed as fictions.

26

Sandra visited Pat in the afternoon. As she cycled to her house she thought of Josephine. The time had come when a person's actions took on a hard, permanent edge. School and her friends there were gone. Like dawn it didn't last. Now, the sun was out and the light everywhere. There were no softening tricks of the imagination. Josephine had dragged her malice, as well as Pat's unhappiness into the harsh light.

Mrs. Edwards was sitting at the kitchen table. When she heard her rap, she looked up, smiled, and said, "Come Sandra." She looked composed and serene, as if nothing was wrong. Indeed, the only time Sandra had seen Mrs. Edwards lose her composure was the afternoon when the news of the burning down of Water Street in February 1962 reached Pheasant. It was mid-afternoon, the compound was peaceful, the maids were preparing to take the children for their walks, the factory workers were about to change their shifts, the overseers, including Mr. Edwards, were about to go home to cool showers, cups of tea and newspapers on the verandah. She and Pat were lying on the grass, under the dwarf jacaranda tree. It was quiet, only the breeze and their relaxed conversation, with an occasional noise from one of the houses, something dropped on the floor or a door slammed. From the Edwards' house, the front door banged open. They looked up to see Mrs. Edwards rush out to the landing, her eyes wide and panic-stricken. She looked all around and did not see them. Her hands covered her face. She ran down the front stairs, her skirt flying in the breeze. She shouted twice, "God help us! Water Street burning!" She ran as if she was running to safety then suddenly she stopped, looked around, saw them watching her, and the panic on her face cleared slowly. It was her husband, Mr. Edwards, she was looking for, hoping to see him on his way home from work, though they never got on, hardly spoke. She walked towards them but stopped half way and said as if in a dream, "Whole of Water Street burning. When the firemen tried to put out the fires, the crowd shoot them." Pat did not go to her mother. They did not know how to comfort her. She never encouraged tenderness and even if they could have shared the terror inside them with her, she did not allow it to happen - she just turned and returned to the house. A little later Pat had run up to the house to get the radio and they remained glued to it the rest of the afternoon: shops burnt, damaged, looted, market stalls damaged and looted too, people injured, some killed.

Now Mrs. Edwards was as calm and collected as ever. "How are you? Mummy and Daddy all right?"

"Yes. Pat in?"

She waved towards Pat's bedroom. "Go through."

Pat was lying on her bed, an open book turned face down on her stomach.

"Josephine came this morning," she told her.

"Josephine Marks? What she wanted?"

"She had worries. Money worries, university worries, parents..."

"Josephine has worries?" Pat retorted. "Josephine don't have worries."

"You sound as hard as she."

Pat sat up. "Don't compare me with Josephine. Josephine is a wretch."

"She wants to go to university. Her father won't give her the money."

Pat laughed. "Don't bother with Josephine. Dad knows her old man. He's just like Josephine, like to make his influence felt. He will give her the money, when it pleases him. Josephine like the drama."

"She was in a state."

"She putting it on, to get your sympathy. That family is a joke."

Sandra went to the window and looked out. Mrs. Edwards kept an immaculate garden. A small square lawn was set in the centre of the space behind the house. Flowers bordered the lawn. Wiri-wiri trees and rows of corn grew behind the flower beds. Beyond them there were larger trees: guava, paw-paw, gooseberry and dwarf coconut. Order was important to Mrs. Edwards. Pat tried constantly to live up to her expectations, as Josephine tried to live up to those of her parents. Sandra's own

28

family was not as well off as the Marks or the Edwards, but Helen had expectations of her too.

She turned back to face Pat. She was sitting cross-legged on the bed, reading her book. "Listen," Sandra called.

"Mmh?"

"You listening?"

"Yes!"

"When Josephine came, the old lady behaved so badly."

Pat looked up, frowning. "Badly? Your old lady?" She chuckled. "She threw her out?"

"No, the opposite. She made a fuss, treated her like an honoured guest, bow and scrape..."

"To Josephine...?"

"Yes."

Pat gave her a critical, worried look. "What you getting at?"

She turned away to look at the ordered garden again. "Sometimes I don't know with Mummy, if she knows what she does..."

Pat's laugh sounded uncomfortable. "Of course she knows. What are you getting on with? You being too hard."

People being hard, people being a joke: everyone had their own opinion about that. Now she was being hard too.

"I wish my mother could get what she wants from life."

Pat said softly. "People always want the impossible. That's life. What your old lady wants? Your old people happier than mine. They don't quarrel like mine."

"The grass always greener on the other side."

"I know what I talking about, you hear?"

"When my parents get ready they don't talk to each other for half the year. Talk about ice-cold behaviour. I can't see your parents behaving like that."

"My old man is like that, when he gets ready. Doesn't stay cold for half a year, but long enough to freeze up the whole house and make everybody as miserable as possible."

"There's no need for you to make such heavy weather of it. You sound like is the end of the world with you. When

29

you're leaving?"

"Two months time. A long time."

Pat laughed. "Two months is no time. You intend to stretch it out?"

She sighed. "I feel worried. What about you? You applied for jobs yet?"

Pat shook her head. "Who's going to employ me? With four 'O' levels?"

"Don' talk like that. You haven't tried."

"I don't have brains, like you and Josephine."

Here was another issue: brains. People were hard, a joke, or had or didn't have brains. Who was the authority on these things?

"You talk like Helen. As if brains is something God give some, and not others," she accused Pat.

"I don't know who give it. I know I in' got it."

Pat had decided long ago that she didn't have brains, since they started high school. She excelled at sports. A year ago, she toured the islands with the national basketball team. She was the star player. That came to an end with the onset of G.C.E. exams. Mrs. Edwards put her foot down. Worried that Pat would fail, she ordered her to give up sports, completely. The national coach came to plead with her. Mrs. Gossai, the sports mistress lent her support. The headmaster threw his weight in with Mrs. Edwards. He said he had no time for anyone who wouldn't put education first. No one could tell what Pat felt. She wanted to obey her mother. One day Pat was captain of hockey, basketball and tennis; the next, she wasn't. Then she did badly at her exams. Now, she did nothing but help around the house. She said she would never take up sports again.

Every Sunday, their mothers met at church. They had God and flowers in common. They talked about their gardens and church affairs. Sandra would always carry a picture of them in her mind: of a Sunday, after Harvest mass, the church filled with fruit and coconut palms. The singing was extra robust. The two women always chatted at the church door, long after the rest of the congregation had left, she and Pat waiting at the church gate. This Sunday, the poui tree near the path was shedding yellow blossoms. As the women came along the path, the blossoms tumbled to their hats and shoulders. They brushed them away, treading on the soft carpet formed by the fall.

Pat had fallen in love once, with Michael Rohan. That lasted a short time. Mrs. Edwards came home one afternoon to find him there with them. Mrs. Edwards was outraged; how dare he come to visit without permission; what would the neighbours think, he with two young girls in her house, without a chaperone; besides, his father was only a clerk at a store. Michael stood up for himself, declaring she had no right to talk like that about him, or his father. Afterwards, Pat came home with her. She cried until her eyes were red. Later, Mr. Edwards came to get her. She locked herself into the bathroom. Only after much pleading did Pat emerge, her face puffy from crying. Pat was not morose, nor without 'brains'. She had strength and determination. When she ran in the school races, she was always yards in front. On sports day, she swept the prizes. The school teams which she captained won the tennis, hockey and basketball matches. But she was modest. She did not do it to win. She enjoyed the effort. Sandra's own success in the classroom was tied up with Pat's on the sports field. On sports day, Sandra prowled the edges of the tracks, scowling at the opposition. Similarly, it was Pat who became nervous and anxious at the Debating Society sessions, fussing over and grooming her. In the teeth of competition, they took up each other's emotions, anxieties and fears. Their parents and teachers saw it but thought it irrelevant. They had to achieve according to the rules of competition: every man for himself and the best man wins. It was the chief maxim at school, the ruling ethic of life. Myrna Chandler said this often enough. Sandra once overheard Myrna's comment to another teacher: "Pat Edwards is weak." It stung as much as Josephine's laughter at the Edwards's unhappiness. It was arrogant. It made her begin to distrust Myrna's teaching.

She suggested, "Pat, I have an idea. Why not try to find a job in Georgetown? We could live together, get a flat."

Pat laughed till her eyes watered. When she composed herself, she fixed Sandra with a sad, grave look. "Girl, where you come from? You know what you're saying? You know what people would say about two young women living by themselves in Georgetown? They would say we're sharking. You know what 'sharking' means? It mean 'looking for man', out for a good time. They have worse words for it."

"Lord, it seem everything a person wants, something bad goes with it. But I tell you, I make up my mind. From now, I don't give a rusty cent what anybody thinks about me. If I'm sure what I'm doing is the best, I'm going to do it. All that nonsense is just to keep a woman down, keep them in their place."

Pat looked amazed. "Well yes! You getting bold! Laying down your own rules and regulations! Try!"

"So what you're going to do with your young life then?"

Pat shook her head. She wanted to end the talk. She returned to her book. They were more apart nowadays. These days brought no new event, but within herself, Sandra knew she was changing, and everyone was changing in her eyes. She would not get closer to Pat, Ben, Helen and T than she was now. Being at home and they accepting her there, she liked the feeling of closeness with them, of no longer being a child among them. This two month interval before Georgetown was a short time, Pat said. But it was too short.

Sitting quietly with Pat, Sandra was sorry their childhood and girlhood were at an end, that their conversation just now had to happen. They were going separate ways, with Pat turning her back on independence, and she confronted by it. They shared a childhood and girlhood. Did women share womanhood? When they looked at the future now, the questions brought a wall down between them. It stretched and strained their bond. Pat lay on her side, her arm supporting her head as she read, nonchalant. She wanted to tell Pat her fears, but she would not understand.

Outside, the villages were quiet. Life was going on. People were working hard for their living, for bread and butter. The wheels and cogs of the factory were turning. What did questions

32

about youth, separation and changes matter? Why did these things complicate life? Did Pat know she was hurling away her child's mask and donning a harsh woman's face, lips set in a pout, her body taut with self-inflicted silence, reading and not reading, but losing her thoughts in the book? Pat was saying goodbye in her own way. Go, her silence spoke: you go and face things separately now. She was preparing herself to face her parents' divorce, by herself.

For Pat, growing meant accepting obstacles, frustration and disappointment. She had no defences against her mother. Their relations were strict, formal and ordered. Pat took orders, and did not complain. There was no discussion. Was Pat becoming like her mother? The thought alarmed Sandra, jolted and rooted her to the present.

"I'm going," she told Pat. "Let me know if you decide to work."

"I don't think I will, yet. I want to be with my parents."

"Forever?"

Pat shrugged, smiled wryly, and assumed her most impenetrable expression.

Ben closed the shop on Sunday afternoons and went to sleep in the hammock under the guinep tree. On one of those afternoons, when Helen was cleaning the shop, she had found his aging accounts. They were stacked a dozen high, each a thick foolscap book. Their spines fell away easily, the threads melted loose. His handwriting hadn't changed over the years. Customers' unpaid debts dated back seventeen years, carried forward to the current books, uninterrupted by sub-totals, under lengthy columns headed 'Items' on the left, 'Prices' on the right. Many accounts were crossed out with the word DECEASED, in large block letters. When she totalled the acounts, the accumulated debts ranged from sums of one hundred to a few thousand dollars.

Helen commented, "Your Daddy in' no businessman."

Deep in sleep, his left leg dangled over the side of the hammock. His arms were crossed on his stomach. He lay in a twisted position, his head almost touching his shoulder. His mouth was half-open, and the breeze played with his thinning hair. The sunlight finding its way through the leaves of a tree, flecked the length of his body with drops of light.

"I weary quarrel with him," Helen said. "Them ladies only got to smile with him, and he would hand them the whole shop. And when I talk about it they call me a virago. He like to give them credit. It is not business, is pleasure."

Ben had come to the kitchen. He saw his books brushed clean, she still at work on the figures. He was resentful. He demanded bitterly, "Who gave you permission to interfere with my books?"

He wanted no apology. He was hurt. Instead of being pleased, he felt betrayed. Later, he burnt the accounts. Before that, he sulked for days, and wouldn't speak to them.

At home, Ben and Helen were not like individuals, but combatants in a battlefield. They fought over their beliefs. Their friends took sides. Helen was pro-Georgetown and all that implied. Ben was pro-Pheasant and all that implied. No quarter was given. Helen was pro-education, Ben anti. He loved the village and the people. Apart from her close circle of friends, Helen hated the village. Their friends were not so much involved in their quarrels as concerned with protecting them from each other, each group close, loyal and indivisible.

Helen, Nurse, Miss K, Noor and Zena bound themselves together. They prided themselves on their independence of mind. Had they had opportunities, they felt, they would have done better. Their postures were bold. With each other, they let down their guard and were subtle and humorous. They lived in a world of their own, shutting out and barricading their lives against the reality that they lived in a place where their fates were confined by poverty. Restless, they built little rebellious dramas into each day.

As a girl, Nurse Nathaniel had worked at the village hospital. When it was shut down she went to the the town hospital. She was now retired, but served the village. Whenever she visited, her laughter rang deep and frequent through the house. In the grip of mirth, she threw her head back, and let it rock her body. On Christmas days, at christenings and weddings, she would accept a shot of rum, asking the Lord to forgive her before she downed it. In her presence, the men took off their hats, and the women watched their tongues. Whose children she had delivered, who she had seen to death's door: this was their regular source of conversation. She was a large woman who liked to wear striped and check dresses with small round collars, reminiscent of her nurse's uniform.

Nurse, like Noor, was the kind of woman who, it seemed to Sandra, possessed the kind of strength she would like to have. Yet they were different on the outside. Nurse was Afro-Guianese and Noor was Indo-Guianese. Nurse was an Anglican and Noor was a Hindu. Nurse was a trained nurse out in the world, up and down the road on her cycle every day, in and out of each home, giving advice, prescribing cures and treatments, and Nurse did not distinguish between the races. If you were sick and in need, she came at any hour, however large or small, physical or mental the problem. Noor exerted the same influence though she was uneducated, without Nurse's sort of training. Noor was especially skilled at settling severe family and marital conflicts. Husbands and wives in crisis went to her for advice. In her gentle presence they became humble and tolerant. Daughters who threatened suicide and violent sons were taken to Noor who invariably adopted them in some form or other, became a surrogate mother. Noor and Nurse exchanged experiences when they met. Nurse's husband had died many years ago and her only son, James, had grown up and gone to live in Georgetown where he was now working as a male nurse in the Public Hospital. Noor was childless. Her husband, Muniram, was a boiler at the factory. Each afternoon, Noor and Muniram could be seen sitting together on their landing, sipping a cup of tea and chatting in a relaxed way, like old friends.

Miss K did people's washing for a living. She travelled from Forest to Corentyne to the town, to various homes, spending a day in each, and while doing the washing and ironing, impress-

35

ing with her sharp wit and sarcasm. She hated men; when not belittling them, she was subtle and soft-spoken. She wore head-cloths which she wrapped in various fashions, and chewed tobacco discreetly. She was always thanking the Lord for the shelter over her head and her daily plate of food, which, she said, were all a woman needed, as long as she "di'n bother with no foolish man". People said that Miss K was married once, but the man had gone away and never come back.

Zena's husband had a woman in town. She was also child-less. Like Miss K, she hated men. Her husband's unfaithfulness was a constant source of pain which only rum, aspirins and occasional rage-letting appeased. She tracked the woman down once and administered a beating, which only hardened her husband's attitude to her. Ben said she was the only woman in the village who knew how to cook. She was always bringing him small morsels to sample, and this caused a few rows between Zena and Helen.

These women formed a maternal council. They met in Helen's kitchen to solve not only each others' problems but also the problems of the women who sought their advice, with Miss K and Zena adding wit and cynicism for good measure.

Ben and his friends let their individual personalities flow easily into group camaraderie. Some of their friendships dated back to their schooldays. Their conversations were a reaffirma-tion of belonging to each other and their places of work and male authority. The women's talk too was a form of binding, but also a release from their confinement not only as plantation people but also as women at home. They talked to clear a larger place where they could bask in their individuality, briefly, before the demands of family claimed them again.

Apart from Helen, they deemed Ben kind. Men and women from the other villages came to tell him their troubles. That, said Helen, was because they could get things from him, because they knew he was happy to give away what he had. He knew no other life but Pheasant. The men stopped in on their way to the factory and canefields to get a packet of cigarettes, and they stopped in again on their way home, but lingered for talk and companionship.

In Ben's and Helen's battles, ends were never spoken of, only means: the ways of doing things, of living. Sandra overheard these quarrels, and thought them futile. It achieved nothing, only set them further apart.

Ben's friends were his clients, and they had devised, over the years, a system to accomodate their dual relationship. He never kept a written record of their credit. "Ben, ah take a beer. That make twenty this week." Or, "Ben, that make twenty pack a' cig'rette this week, and eight four cents loaf bread, an' about five stout." To this kind of rough estimating they assented, and settled at the end of the month to their mutual satisfaction. Helen said it used to drive her crazy when she first came to live in Pheasant, but she had got used to it. It did not mean she accepted it; it was madness; he didn't do it to make a living, only to pass the time of day. Ben had his retorts ready, some as sarcastic as Helen's. He told her to mind her own business and keep her place; her job was to keep the children fed and house clean, clothes washed and food cooked; how he ran his business was his business; he provided the children's school fees; when Christmas came he could hand her money to buy new curtains and new furniture if she wanted these; he bought her clothes; so why did she want to tell him how to run his business; she should count her blessings, go down on her knees and thank God - instead of harassing him night and day; as if he wasn't good enough for her; let her leave him and find another man. The invitation to leave and find another man always silenced Helen, though inwardly she raged.

They had the ability to make their children feel they were the cage which forced them into cohabitation; yet, they put them first, in their different ways. To Ben, his children's happiness was important. They must live at peace with themselves, their conscience must be clear, no one must insult them; the law of life was learning to live with people according to the rules of conscience. This made no sense to Helen. Her classic reply was: could one eat and drink these things; did it keep away starvation, pay the doctor's bills? She was ambitious for her children, but Ben undermined her aims. For Helen, their redemption lay in education, but Ben called them away from 'the damn homework' to help him with a chore he thought more important. He cut himself off from them unless they did what he wanted them to do. As the children grew older, moulded by school, they found themselves cut off from him, and therefore from the village itself, stranded in their own orbit where they had to find their own way, pushed by Helen towards a vague 'better future'. To grow was to fight her parents' battles. Sometimes Sandra was afraid of it, more often, she could not imagine anything else. She had to swim her way through their turbulence.

"I could have become a nurse," Helen always reminded him. "I always had ambition. You have none. You are more like my mother, like Sarah. I see people come from poverty and make good. But not you. You think you can do better than people like that. The Roman Catholic priests and nuns use to beg Sarah to let me become a nurse. They say they would pay my way, look after me, but Sarah say no. I dared not open my mouth to tell her I want it. I use to pray she would agree, but no, when I finish primary school, she drag me to her stall in Stabroek every day to help her. If I had power over my life, I wouldn't be here behind God back with you. I would be living in a civilised place, like Georgetown."

When Ben had no answer to her tirades, he resorted to stony silence, and sought out his friends for consolation. They had the power to give him peace. Only goodwill flowed between them. They had no secrets, trusted each other and were proud of it. Helen did not understand how these things could make a person happy. She said he and his friends fitted each other like a hand in a glove, that she didn't know why they didn't marry each other then they could sit and talk whole day and whole night. One of these friends reappeared after an absence of ten years. He was a short grey-haired man. When Ben saw him get off the bus, he'd exclaimed:

"Well, what is this I seeing? Is Reuben I seeing?"

Reuben was amused by Ben's surprise. They couldn't get

enough of shaking hands and hugging each other.

"Man Reuben," Ben said, "I thinking all this time that tiger done eat you out in the interior. Remember when you lef'? Tellin' me you goin' porkknockin'? An' I ask you if you in' frighten, li'l piece man like you goin' an' porkknockin' - that dem Amerindian people chase you with bow and arrow...?"

"Man Ben," Reuben replied, "I married an Amerindian gal."

"What! Well now I know why you like the place! Congrats man, congrats..."

"An' I have three children, jus' like you."

"Well yes, I never thought you would marry and settle down. You was always such a serious fellow."

"An' I in' still serious?"

With each exchange, they laughed deeply. Ben introduced Helen to Reuben, and he complimented him on his choice. He stayed all day. He talked about the interior.

"You never see so much land," Reuben said. "Cattle fat fat fat."

Reuben spoke with contentment about the interior. With his hands he described the size of the pumpkins that grew on his farm. Ben described the changes in Pheasant, and Reuben replied that he had noticed: more people, more houses, cars, buses, a police station, and he had seen an electricity generator in someone's yard.

They talked like ancient men, referring to the vanished world of their childhood, not the recent past. It was the first time Sandra heard Ben criticise Pheasant, confess to someone that changes he felt apprehensive about were taking place: mechanization on the estate, the growing influence of the Georgetown unions and hints of conflict spreading from the capital unlike anything before. She saw it was the very distant past his values were based on, not the present.

Ben, Reuben and Joe Bachan, who still lived in Good Land, had been schoolboys together in Canefields. Their parents were indentured labourers and the children of freed slaves. Their parents did not survive to be middle-aged. Lacking contact with the towns, the modern towns, centres of business, education and colonial power, where the influence of the English was strongest, living in such a deeply rural area, so close to their own past, submerged in the life and landscape of the plantation and the forest, completely segregated from the English overseers, wedded entirely to their own ragged community, they were men who preferred to hold back from the future. They did not trust it at all, did not like it, the brashness, ignorance and arrogance of it, although their instinct for freedom was as fierce and strong as anybody else's. Cactus, who still lived in the forest, belonged to their parents' generation, and their stand resembled his. This rush to the town, the rush to be modern without understanding what it meant - men like them treated the future like a plague. It was typical of Reuben not to go to town but to the interior.

Days after Reuben left, Ben repeated everything he said, word for word. It all vindicated his philosophy. "You see how Reuben does live?" he told Helen. "I in' tell you a man could live without hustling, fighting an' losing he pride?"

When Sandra had finished primary school, sat and passed her high school entrance examinations, it had brought on their worst quarrel. Helen asked him to make provision for her school fees. Ben declared he was against the idea of her going to high school. It was not money, he said, but principles; he thought education was a waste of time; besides, she didn't consult him about it; she just went ahead and made plans for the children without him; he was just a money-making machine; now she wanted money for the school fees, only now was he to be involved.

They quarrelled for days. The tension mounted. Their exchanges grew more fierce, until, one night, Helen threw an ice-pick at him. It barely missed him, landing in the wall a few inches from his head. It happened quickly. In the instant it took Helen to realize what she had done, all their blood-boiling fury went. Sandra saw, for the first time, the purest look of intimacy pass between them. They saw, at its deepest, their capacity for destruction. In that second, the distinction between the attacker and the victim blurred. Both were guilty, and saw it. Their faces mirrored one conscience. But it couldn't last. Their natures could not alter shape and direction now, after a lifetime of battles. Ben recovered from the shock. He shook with rage. He gritted his teeth and clenched his fists. Helen said nothing. She only turned and fled the house, leaving him without means to vent his rage. Then he too stormed from the house, leaving them to complete the chores, light the lamps and shut the shop. He returned when they were asleep. When he was settled in bed, Sandra rapped on his door and asked after Helen. He said she was in New Amsterdam, spending the night with the Shepherds. Mr. Shepherd was headmaster of the primary school, another old friend of his, the only one Helen approved of, the one who lived for the future.

Next afternoon, Helen returned with Mr. Shepherd. Sandra saw them get off the bus, and ran to tell Ben. But when she approached him, her confidence left her: she had to stay out of it, these were adult passions. She withdrew, but watched from the doorway. Ben, sitting near the counter, did not see them until Mr. Shepherd loomed over him.

"Good afternoon, Ben," Mr. Shepherd said.

When Ben was hurt, he carried his wound visibly. He gave Helen a bitter look as she lifted the counter flap and entered confidently, as if she had committed no crime.

"Good afternoon, Shep," Ben replied, reluctant.

Mr. Shepherd wore his grey suit, with the jacket open, so his suspenders could be glimpsed. He had the habit of clearing his throat and baring his teeth before speaking. He did so now.

"Man Ben," he said. "What Helen telling me now?"

Ben sat rigid. He was struggling to control himself. He kept his eyes on Helen. She chatted with the customers and straightened the sweet bottles on the counter.

"Ben, we have to talk about this thing, man," Mr. Shepherd insisted. "Helen tell me you don't want to send Sandra to high school."

Ben broke his silence. "I don' believe in education."

"What?" Mr. Shepherd was shocked. "You don't believe in what?"

The customers, hearing the alarm in Mr. Shepherd's voice, pricked up their ears.

Mr. Shepherd sighed. "Ben, I know you pride yourself on being a self-made philosopher, but sometimes you go a li'l too far..."

"Don' worry criticise me..."

Mr. Shepherd waved his arms, and interrupted sharply, "No no, man, we in' talkin 'bout you, we talkin' 'bout Sandra. Don' be so damn selfish....!"

"Selfish?" Ben retorted. "Who bein' selfish? I should know the meaning of the word better than any man. I always put my children first. Don' come to me with 'selfish', Shep. When you use that word, it depend on what a man talkin' 'bout wanting..."

"Ben, don't complicate and confuse this story! You know very well what we talking about. We talking about education! Let us talk education, not philosophy. Don' shake up the two things in one bottle. Everything belong in it place. Now you hear me out! Listen, this is not our time. This is modern times. In our days you lucky if you got the chance to get an education. Now, all our children could get an education. You could be excused for turning your back on it. It was too bleady hard in those days. You and I went to school together. You had to mind your family when your father died. I admire you for it, at fourteen starting a business and succeeding in building one. I went on to teach and study some more, and I had was to starve just like you. By the sweat of our brow we two survive and make good.

But things have changed in this country. We couldn't dream of what these children today could dream of. The children of today are the leaders of tomorrow. And for the first time, it is our responsibility to prepare them for this task. You and I could ever think of running country? Awright, we di'n have that privilege, but we can have it through the children..."

"Girl children run country?" Ben retorted scornfully. "Girl children must stay home and mind children and their

42

home."

Mr. Shepherd's face fell. "Ben, you make me shame. Think! Think! Use the brains God give you. Educate your child and let her be a pride to you. When it come to education, all that matter is brains. I don' see the difference between boy and girl children. Education is pride, man. Is not something you could eat like a plate a' food, is something higher in satisfaction. Man, when I go to church to pray, is the pride I does thank God for that I get from education."

Ben was outraged. "Pride! Education! What about Care? I mus' send my child 'way from her home whole damn day? Look man, if something happen to her in town, who would care? Not a damn soul! Town people don' care 'bout one another. Is pure dog eat dog does go on in town. Besides, nobody don't have interest in a child like it own parents! I know them primary school teachers here, I know their parents, the kind of homes they come from, whethe' they is decent people or not. I mus' entrus' my child to town people I don't know?"

Mr. Shepherd's feelings were hurt. "Awright, Ben. So much for me. I is town people. Now I know what you think about me."

Ben repented. "I in' talkin' 'bout you, man Shep. You is different. You live among us. Your spirit here. I talkin' 'bout these young people I see put here. I talkin' 'bout these young people I see them put here to teach, with no full experience of life and no maturity. Ol' time teachers that teach me and you was mature, reliable people."

The talk exhausted them both. Mr. Shepherd turned to chat with the customers. Helen, bold now, was moving freely about the shop, passing close by Ben, brushing him with her skirt. He seemed to have forgotten their quarrel. When Mr. Shepherd left, he went to the kitchen, and sat alone near the window for a long while. She followed him there, and tried to distract him from his thoughts. He resisted stoically.

Helen spent one day in Georgetown making plans for Sandra to live with Daphne. She returned on the last bus. "It arranged," she declared, dropping into a chair, shedding her spike-heeled shoes. "Daphne say Sandra lucky to get a reporter job. Jobs not easy to come by. Daphne has a nice cottage in Regent Street, the quiet end, far from the shops. Georgetown bright! I walk an' walk an' fill me eyes. If you see cloth in Fogarty's!"

"How Daphne?" Ben asked.

Sandra remembered Daphne from her visit many years ago: she was tall and thin, and wore a black dress and a wide-brimmed straw hat with a spray of plastic flowers stuck in the band. Daphne sent Christmas cards every year. They were always inscribed: "To my beloved cousin Ben, and his family. From Daphne."

"Daphne all right," Helen replied. "You know she was always all right. Her parents left her plenty money. She ask after you, and send howdy. She as stuck up as ever. Everything is Ben this, Ben that. She don' talk to me 'bout nothing else."

"Don' bad talk the woman. She boarding and lodging Sandra."

"At seventy-five dollars a month! Lord, look, if wasn't for Sandra, I wouldn't go into her house."

Sandra couldn't hold her tongue. "But you expect me to go live with her," she commented.

They both turned a reproachful look on her. Ben was reconciled to her departure.

"Show me you got muscles," T challenged, handing Sandra a paddle.

T only stroked the water with the paddle and the canoe surged along in a perfect, straight line along the river. They stroked the water faster, gathered speed, and moved further into the depths of the forest. When she was tired, she sat at the front and leaned forward, enjoying the sensation of racing along on the surface of the deep, surging body of water. The forest roused sensation and feeling. The sky, the wilderness of thousands of huge, entangled trees, the river, all signified a vast, unchartable and infinite mystery. It made the world of home and school insignificant.

"Faster!" she urged T, but he only laughed and splashed her with water. He stopped near a horde of sleeping alligators, threw empty tin cans at them and emitted blood-curdling screams which sent the creatures splashing and slithering into the depths.

When he tired, he let the boat drift along. "So you going away," he commented.

She nodded. When his father lost a leg at the factory and could not mind the family, T and Estelle had come to live with them for two years. During that time, they became close friends.

Sakiwinkis burst leaves off branches in their flight through the forest, and the pheasants, strange, ancient-looking birds, curved a dipping path in and out of the trees. There were large intervals of silence here; you could feel the space open and shut round you. When it opened, it took you into its silence and snuffed out the life you brought with you; when it shut itself, it was like a flower closing, keeping the secret of its beauty. Then, it left you without comfort, feeling apprehension, so the sudden bursts of noise that broke like shrieks from its still, closed centre shattered and shredded any sense of calmness.

"So you going away," T repeated.

"You still playing Tarzan?" she taunted.

He laughed. "You don' come see we at all since you turn high school lady. An' when you do come, you mockin' we, callin' people Tarzan.

"Who tell you to live behind God back?" she teased.

He changed the subject. "You brother, Jay, come he' with some town friends a Sunday, say I mus' give them a ride in me boat. Dem fellows bring air gun. I give them me boat an' tell them go 'long. Dem boys ruction bad. They shoot Cactus duck, tek am fo' wil' duck. Up to today, I pass Cactus upcreek, an' he stan' up 'pon he bank an' cuss me upside down. I had was to tell them boys don' come back he' with no air gun. Cactus live he' long befo' anybody else, an' he don' trouble a soul."

"Dem boys young and wild," she commented.

45

"Eh? Well try tell dem they mus' go look fo' wildness in cinema."

"T boy, like this is the last time I breathing creek air."

"You talkin' like you goin' dead."

As with Pat, she could no longer talk with him. She was beginning to appreciate that when people no longer shared the same experiences, they easily lost patience and interest in each other. Departure and its attendant feelings interested neither Pat nor T. They couldn't cope with it. They were used to closeness and familiarity with her. Anything that changed that was a source of irritation, not something to understand together. She couldn't expect them to share her thoughts. They couldn't say 'Go' without sourness or resentment.

"T, what you going to do with you'self?"

"Who say I going to do anyt'ing that I in' doin' now? I farming as usual. Me in' goin' nowhere like you. Why you don' stay here, whe' everybody know you an' you know them. Why you want go somewhe' whe' you got to depend 'pon Tom, Dick an' Harry?"

"T boy, what work I would do here?"

"Teach."

"And cane children day in day out? Remember how licks used to fly left right and centre at school? No thanks."

"Work in office, clerk work, telephone operator, nurse...plenty work he'..."

"I don' want to do any'a those things. I want to do the job in Georgetown."

"Wha' job Georgetown got we in' got he'?"

"Reporting fo' the newspaper."

"Lady does do tha'?"

"Yes, man."

"An' wha' so nice 'bout it?"

"You learn new, real things all the time. I tired sticking me head in books that got nothing to do with me."

"Lord, all the time you want learn? High school in' enough?"

"Everybody think differently. I have a right to think how I

want to think. People always fighting over opinions. I want to be sure about what I know."

He sighed. "I don' understand. I only know I don' like depend 'pon no man. Education is pure hustle. I hope wha' I see befall some people don' befall you. Look, you know Prem? The fellow pass G.C.E. with plenty subjects. He apply fo' teachin' job at primary school, an dem people tell he to turn Christian first. Prem father is pundit. How people could even t'ink to ask he to change religion to get job? Is real eye-pass. An' Joan, Mr. James, the guttersmith daughter, pass G.C.E. too. She go to police station an' ask fo' clerk work. The sergeant give she belly instead a' work. She had to sleep with man befo' she get work. Now she gettin' baby. I tell Mr. James he should go down to the station an' buss up deh scamp. The girl stupid, yes, but is anxiety make she do it. Me, I want work fo' me, not to please no man. Only t'ing control my life," T spread open his arms, "when sun shine or rain fall."

"Well I wish you luck. I hope you always feel like that if it make you happy."

You try an' live how make you happy too. Don' let no damn man control y'u life."

"Man musn't control you life? Only sun and rain? How so, man?"

"Sun and rain stay like me: wild and own way. I know all it ways. Men, only God know what nex' they would t'ink up to do to one another, what mischief an' nastiness. I wan' keep my faith in life. You try. You t'ink you strong? You in' know man stronger than woman?"

"Who say so?"

"I say so." He pointed to the spot where the alligators had been sleeping. "I know man can fight alligator, kill alligator, even camudi, an' live. But I don' think woman could."

"Tha's not the only kinda strength people could have." She pointed to her head. "What about mental strength?" She placed the palm of her hand over her breast. "And strength of the heart. Heart and head. Not just physical strength." She smiled. "You have all three, T. Give me a chance, man."

47

He looked at her thoughtfully. He sighed. "You think you is man."

She laughed and shook her head. "So only man could do what he like?"

He nodded. "Yes. Man would never let woman do everything man could do. I bet you would never meet a man like tha'. He would always keep you down. No man don' like woman better than he, or even like he."

"You never know."

"Especially in Georgetown. You is stranger in Georgetown. Man would like you because you is woman only, no other reason. Anyt'ing else they would t'ink you making trouble, trying to make them look small."

There was a warning in his voice she did not want to hear. He was going to remind her of Wismar 1963, what happened to Indo-Guianese women there; he was going to tell her that they would kill her in Georgetown, like the people who were killed in the race riots there. Those fears did not bother her. If you lived by race in this country it killed you one way or the other - you either stifled in your own narrow inwardness or you engaged in conflict. There had to be another way. T's way was one way, to go back in time, literally, like Cactus, the free slave who liked to call everybody slaves. T was trying to tell her she would only be a slave in Georgetown, a slave to men.

She tried to bring them back to their own ground. "Good women like Noor and Nurse: you want to tell me they not strong?"

"Nurse and Noor not young like you and they stay with their own people all their life. That make them strong."

"So is not being man that make you strong? So is woman staying with her own kind make her strong."

"All two."

At T's house, his father lay in the hammock. His hair was completely grey. He greeted her, "Sandra, beti, how you do?"

"Sandra goin' live in Georgetown," T told him.

48

His look changed from warmth to indifference. "You goin' to Georgetown? Try, people ruction bad the'."

"Whe' Estelle?" T asked. "Sandra want see she befo' she go."

"Estelle upstairs."

"Estelle!"

Estelle came down, and seeing her, leaped on her and spun her round. T watched them cynically.

"Awright, Estelle," he cautioned. "Stop you stupidness now. You see how big woman like you still playful? Sandra goin' an lef'in' we. She going to Georgetown."

"Eh? What story this?"

T put his arm round Estelle. "Sandra, watch Estelle he'. You see she? She want turn town girl." He turned to Estelle. "Not true? One bad man she go married. Day an' night he beatin' she black and blue. She can' handle he. I had was to go an' trash he in he own house. The man is a murderer."

Estelle pushed him away, turned her back on them, and folded her arms.

T continued, "Now she want go an' work in store in New Amsterdam. You know them whore house over them store in Grey Street? You know how them whore turn whore? They lef' them good house in country, say they goin' work in store in town. Then they get promotion upstairs. Estelle want turn whore. Sandra, watch y'u ol' playmate. She want turn whore."

Estelle flew at him. She flayed him with her fists. When he grabbed her arms, she kicked his legs. Her face was wet with tears. When he let her go, she swept a stick from the ground and lifted it to strike him.

"Estelle!" he yelled, crouching, his eyes filled with fear.

She froze, breathing hard, staring at him. It was the same look that passed between Ben and Helen the night she had thrown the ice pick at him. They had driven their frustration and unhappiness to a pitch where their emotions ruled reason. When it brought them to danger point, when it was clear they could threaten life as it threatened them, they brought it to a halt.

49

Purged of rage, they reclaimed their reason.

Estelle threw the stick tamely at him.

They waited at the roadside for the bus. Estelle sulked, and T sat on a tree stump and pelted bricks into the water.

"Well," T said, when the bus arrived. "You make sure you come back and see us folks now and then. Don't forsake us."

"Take care Estelle."

"Walk good," Estelle returned.

Three weeks before she was due to leave, Josephine arrived with a stranger. Helen ran upstairs to warn her. "Josephine come, with a strange fellow." She met them on the landing.

"I want you to meet a friend," Josephine declared. "David Petrie."

He was very serious, tall and immaculately dressed in a white long-sleeved shirt, dark blue tie and trousers, black shoes highly polished. He nodded stiffly and shook her hand. Indoors, he merely listened while she and Josephine made small talk. Josephine announced she was leaving for the United States in a week, and wanted Sandra to come to her house that night as a farewell occasion. She went downstairs to ask Helen's consent, then Josephine followed a little later, to say goodbye to Ben and Helen. When they were alone, David Petrie spoke:

"You and Josephine have known each other a long time?"

"Yes, since school."

He said nothing else. He had the air of an older man. He thought before he spoke, keeping a detached expression. Ben prided himself on his self-control, but David Petrie's brand of this was different. It was decided he would return at eight to take her to Josephine's.

She was in her room, getting dressed, when he arrived. Helen's sewing machine stopped going when his voice sounded.

Ben came to the door and rapped.

"Sandra?"

"Come in."

"You going to Josephine with that fellow?"

"Yes. You knew. You said it was o.k."

"Mr. and Mrs. Marks goin' be there?"

"Yes."

She was ready to go, but he hung in the doorway. He was worried, not sure about David Petrie.

She said, "I will come home early."

"How you coming home? I could send Mitch fo' you."

"Don' do that. He will bring me back."

"You sure?"

"I will be alright."

David Petrie rose when she came out, and held open the front door. All the family were stiff and self-conscious as they watched them leave.

"It's so dark," he complained, as they descended the steps.

When they were in the car, he asked her, "You live here all your life?"

"Yes."

"I'm from Trinidad. B.G. very different."

As they drove along, he gripped the wheel and peered ahead intensely. He sighed or grunted when a car approached. "Lord, man, these people never hear about dipping headlights?" he fretted. A beetle was trapped inside the windscreen. Angry, he slapped it and it fell, dead, to the dashboard. "These insects!" he complained. The bus approached, rattling from out of the darkness like a hundred tin cans. He stopped the car to let it pass, stuck his head out the window, watched it go by, and muttered, "Well, what is this? The devil's chariot heading for Pandemonium?" He turned to her, "This road is a death trap. I bet you have a lotta accidents."

His fussing riled her. "You should check your facts before you say that. I know of only one serious accident that

51

happened here."

"Well, I feel better to hear that. But next time I come I better check to make sure I insured properly. It so dark here. What you find to do here?"

"Just because it's dark, it doesn't follow we do nothing."

He sighed with relief when they came to the smoother, well-lit road.

"When Josephine told me she had a friend here, in the country, I didn't imagine someone like you," he said.

He was trying to regain his poise. She asked, "What you expected? A canecutter?"

He laughed. "This is a hell of a country. Flat, flat. We have hills in Trinidad. The landscape has variety. Port of Spain is a city. Georgetown is a big village. I don't know how Guianese people can live in a place like this..."

"All your hills might make me feel I'm in prison," she countered, "confined, with nowhere to go but the sea all around. And we don't have your hurricane problems."

"I don't feel trapped in Trinidad. I get out you know, and travel about a bit. If you can do that, no need to feel confined."

"That's lucky."

"They say travel broadens the mind."

"It broadened yours?"

"I leave others to judge that."

"Maybe Pheasant can broaden your mind."

He laughed loudly. "I doubt it. I'm a town boy, live in Port of Spain all my life. Very rarely I go to the country. I suppose I don' really like it."

"Neither does my mother."

"She's not from here?"

"No, Georgetown."

"From my point of view, the difference isn't tremendous."

"Doesn't mean to say it isn't for her."

He said nothing else. He seemed to her self-centred. For him, she thought, the possibility that Pheasant was significant to anyone had to be sacrificed to his claims to sophistication. His sophistication was worth something in Trinidad or abroad, but not here. This was the real cause of his annoyance, not the potholes, darkness, reckless driving and insects. But his discomfort was genuine. He lost confidence, and then tried to say things to make himself appear masterful and in command, not seeing that they did the opposite.

He was comfortable at Josephine's house, in the comfortable chairs, with a glass of whisky in his hand, talking business with Mr. Marks. He was an accountant. Josephine was going to study Business Administration at the college where Petrie had studied four years before. He was here to do work for Mr. Marks, and advise Josephine. But he barely got a word in. Whenever he addressed Josephine, Mr. or Mrs. Marks interrupted after the first sentence; they took up an idea and fought over it like two large over-fed pet dogs over a bone, while the younger people sat by, ignored.

To get out of the Marks's house was to feel released from a prison. The freedom was short-lived. Driving alone with a stranger at midnight was just as uncomfortable as the Marks's household. Sandra thought of Ben and of his behaviour earlier. He was suspicious and superstitious about town and town people, as irritated by them as Petrie was irritated by Pheasant. Was it irritation she felt too with the Marks and with Petrie? Did you reject people because they irritated you? Was irritation a proper reason to criticise and belittle a way of life that did not verify the different person you were? Perhaps there must be something inadequate with the person and the life if it felt uncomfortable the moment it contacted a difference.

For her, the darkness outside did not hold a threat. She could close her eyes as the car drove through the familiar villages and by the alternating scents know exactly where she was: where the black sage grew; the canefields; the dank vegetation in a swampy village; the canals smelling of over-ripe and rotting cane and weeds; the sawmill; the jumbie tree in the graveyard, musky

53

and smelling of rotting bark; lawns around the estate compound and cricket pitch; the breeze dropping when they passed through a cramped village, then blowing strong where there was a break and the land lay empty.

Petrie drove past the house in Pheasant. "I hear you have a river along here somewhere," he said.

"Yes, but you can't see it now, in the darkness. You went past the house."

"You get the feeling driving here you could go on driving forever."

He was calm and relaxed, sitting back comfortable in his seat, his fingers lightly controlling the wheel.

"The road ends here."

He stopped the car and switched off the engine. They were near the disused stelling. It was a remnant of the slave plantations, built of solid greenheart logs. The building held echoes which resounded at the least sound: the bats shrieking and flying round the rafters; the alligators slithering through gaps in the flooring and splashing into the depths again; all the rodent and insect life there - her ear picked up the sounds. The river lapped against the banks; its passage could be heard in the darkness as a distant drum, a faint boom from deep in the ground, obscured by layers of earth before it reached them. The dimensions of silence and noise which she knew here by day were more enlarged and profound at midnight.

Petrie lit a cigarette. The spark of the match glinted first like a blade, then exploded into a soft orange flame. It lit his face up like a mask.

Dutch plantations used to be situated along the river here, and slave rebellions were frequent. Those days were gone, but another layer of history had unfolded along the Canje river when indentured labourers had come to the area. The Afro-Guianese who remained were as close to their slave past as the Indo-Guianese to their indentured past. They still knew the names of the ships which had brought them to British Guiana. Africans and Indians shared each other's customs in a way that would be unthinkable elsewhere, and that was probably no longer possible after the race riots. The Jews, Portuguese, French and Dutch had come to Canje too. So close was this past here, it was as if the landscape wore many masks and the spirits of the past still lived here, especially here in the forest where even the silence echoed.

He said, "Driving across a flat land, you get the feeling you're going nowhere. Sometimes, but only sometimes, that could be nice, when you want to escape the madness and the rat race, the competition and the hustling. Endless, endless space. Lord, the country is really empty, the end of civilisation."

"As you know it," she commented.

He laughed softly. "Don't take it so seriously."

He touched her bare shoulder, and she drew away. "I really should be home by now," she said.

"Relax," he said, and touched her again. She drew away again.

When she opened the front door, the streetlight fell in a vague oblong upon Ben. He was sitting in the rocking chair. He rose, muttered, "You come home so late," and went to his bedroom.

In her room, she turned up Sarah's lamp. The mirror caught all the light and held her reflection there: she saw it with David Petrie's eyes. His touch still burnt on her shoulder, imprinted with the warmth of his hand, as warm as the heat from the lamp when she put her hand near the glass shade, the core of energy much too close to flesh. Flesh when blemished was like any other flesh, holding body and soul together. Burnt once, burnt twice, you learned to value it, not treat it casually. Losing yourself in the forest you didn't have to think, the greenness and silence held you together. Losing yourself to flesh like your own, you fell into a different mystery, your own and another's.

Next afternoon he returned. The car pulled up at the roadside. He looked up to the open windows and waved. He came through the front gate. His footsteps were firm as he came up the steps.

He rapped on the door, stuck his head through and asked if he could come in. Before she could answer, he was there, beside the sewing machine. He sat down.

"You're sewing?" he asked.

"As you can see, yes."

He did not say anything for a while, then he spoke quickly, "I was wrong to drive you to the forest last night without asking you, and the things I did and said were wrong too." He paused. "I dont want you to be angry. I want you to promise something. When you get to Georgetown, keep in touch, in case you need any help."

"I'll be fine. I'm staying with my auntie."

Helen came upstairs, and he rose to greet her and shake hands. She stayed a few minutes, making small talk with him, enjoying the company of a town person.

"I from Georgetown you know," she declared, "not here. Born and grew there. I married here, and been here ever since. I glad Sandra going to town. I think it's a better life."

He was at his best behaviour. He didn't comment. He listened while Helen spoke at greater length about Georgetown, and rose and shook her hand again when she left them.

Later, Jay came in. "Hi," he greeted them.

David greeted Jay like a long-lost friend. "Hi man, you're coming from school?" Jay was carrying his guitar. "You play that well?"

Jay strummed a little on the guitar, then David took it and showed what he could do. They talked about music, cricket, films, easily and casually, in between strumming the guitar.

Now Pat appeared at the front door, surprised to see the stranger. Her eyes lit up. He rose and shook her hand. "Pheasant is full of nice surprises," he commented.

"You're living here or visiting?" Pat asked.

"I live in Georgetown," he replied.

"You have a Trinidadian accent," Pat noted.

He was glad his identity was recognised. "You know it?"

"I went there with the basketball team," Pat said.

With that, they settled into a conversation about the game.

He was a fan, and knew the names of players Pat had met there.

When he left, Pat leaned from the window and waved as he drove off. She turned on Sandra, "You sly fox. You been keeping this fellow to yourself?"

"Look, Pat, behave yourself. Don't be so ridiculous."

"Wait, what's this cold fish behaviour? Since when you prudish? You don't see he has polish?

"Grease is not polish."

Pat shook her head, and commented cynically, "The voice of experience."

"He's Josephine's friend. She brought him when she came to say goodbye. She's going away."

"Never mind whose friend he is."

"You're not being serious."

"Stop acting like some prim and proper, frigid, old maid country bumkin. What there is to be serious about?"

"You drop your pride for a man's sake?"

"Pride not involved. You young. He likes you. Stop acting middle-aged, and pretending you're not flattered."

"You mischievous. You know very well you safe and sound locked up in your house. Your mother is more strict than mine, which is not a bad thing sometimes. And remember what Miss K said: trust no man..."

"You hypocrite, then why he's talking with you if you don't trust him?"

"He's very pushy. I can't tell him to get out or not to come back. Stupid to behave like that. No harm talking to someone, but your position should be clear in your head, not confused..."

Pat laughed. "Well! Your brain been working overtime lady! You intend to make up for your old lady's lack of strictness!"

"Mummy head turned too easily by town things."

"Give you some more time and you will be taking her in hand..."

"Stop making smart comments."

"Sandra, you're young!"

"You were the one talking about 'sharking' the other day, about how people quick to say young girls looking for man. You just as crude."

Pat's face fell. "When you grab hold of an idea you don't let go of it. You always piecing things up like a jigsaw. I said that, yes, but is no reason for you to distrust all men. You can't see David is a gentleman?"

"An inconsistent one. He made a pass, after knowing me only a couple of hours."

Pat's eyes widened in amazement. "And what you did? Put on a Miss Prim and Proper act I bet. Don't tell me."

"Pat, stop joking. I worried about you. Staying home addling your brains."

"One day when you old and old maid, you will be sorry you were like this. Wasted opportunities!"

"Don't prophesy about my future."

David Petrie visited every afternoon over the next two weeks. He and Helen talked a great deal. He described the places he had visited, his student days in the United States, the islands, South America. Helen was greatly entertained by it. It took her out of Pheasant. It did the same for Sandra. It was the first time anyone provided an experienced framework to view the outside world with. Her own and Helen's, Ben's, were too subjective. It could be the only real preparation for Georgetown. David brought it here with him, a framework from outside Georgetown, from a world much wider than Georgetown. He soon became familiar, a consoling presence in the household, because he met a need which had been nagging it, that, in a way, nagged the very existence of Pheasant: the pull of the outside world, magnetic though resisted so strongly by people like Ben, who distrusted it precisely because it held so much attraction.

On his last night in Pheasant, before leaving, he said goodbye to the family. Through the window, sitting on the landing, Sandra saw him shake hands with Ben, Helen, Jay and William. She too would be leaving in a few days.

II

Georgetown was another world. To the child from the country, it was a sea of streets, cars and buildings. To the young woman standing outside the station gates, it was a flat, unpromising maze. She consulted Helen's crude map.

The station was at the top of Carmichael Street, Bishop's High School at the bottom. Tall, white paling staves fenced the school. Girls dressed in white shirts and shorts were playing volleyball on the lawn nearest the street. It reminded her of Pat and schooldays. Already that was in the distant past. A bell rang, and girls dressed in panama hats, green uniforms with white blouses streamed outdoors.

The streets were hot and the sharp sunlight slanted onto the pavements. There was no breeze and the movements of people seemed divided between lethargy and purpose. A store keeper, tape measure round his neck, lounged in the shade of a cloth shop. A larger store, lined and packed with bolts of cloth, lit by fluorescent lights, hummed with shop assistants and men in long-sleeved shirts and ties. Beggars and the occasional drunk lounged near a cake shop or restaurant, counting coins and peering in a daze at passers-by. Cars and bicycles passed up and down the wide street in an uneven flow, a congestion of bulky yellow buses and passengers outside Bourda market where shouts and noises echoed vaguely from within the sheltered areas and the stalls spilled out on the pavements and roadside, like advertisements for those within. Loud juke boxes blared from cake shops where youths hung idle in the doorways, staring vaguely or insolently at the life around them, or swayed or did a jig to the music, downing soft drinks or beer, or chewing on a mouthful of the parched nuts or boiled channa advertised on the small blackboards outside the shops.

A woman was sitting on the back steps of the cottage. Her face was lined. Her black hair was streaked with grey and tied back untidily. She was reading the newspaper. A cigarette was clenched between her thin lips. When she saw Sandra, she folded the newspaper, removed the cigarette and smiled.

"You're the girl from Berbice?" she asked. "The mistress tell me you would come. I is deh servant, Amy. I come in two hours every day, one to three o'clock. Come in, sun hot." Her voice was hoarse and cracked.

Amy led the way into the cottage. The rooms were tiny: a small corridor which served as a sitting room; a larger area partitioned by a low wooden wall, comfortable chairs and a coffee table on one side, a dining table with four matching red chairs on the other, and through the doorway lay the small kitchen, lined with rows of shelves packed with jars, bowls, pots, plates and cups. There were two bedrooms. The largest was Daphne's. Amy took Sandra to her room. The walls were painted cream, the paintwork clean though just beginning to crack. The same curtains, plain light green cotton, hung at all the windows.

She put her suitcase on the bed. Amy stood in the doorway, watching her with a friendly grin on her face. "You like metagee?" she asked. "Ah cook metagee."

"I'll eat later, thanks."

"The mistress comes home late, sometimes not till midnight. She has plenty friends you know, not married like herself and they keep each other company.But she say she will come early today, as you coming. She tell me you will be working with the newspapers. That is good work. I use to know some people work there. They say the pay is good. That is important, man. Money don' last in this place. I have plenty children and grandchildren and God only know how we hand-to-mouth. Prices going up every day, school expense, shoes, clothes, this an' that, you know how it is. And a soul need extra cash for one or two pleasures you know, a drink here, a pack cig'rit there, you know how it is. I like your dress. Who made it? Your Mammy? I sew you know. If you want me sew fo' you now and then, I don't charge much."

Amy went from one thing to another, asking many questions, not waiting for replies, puffing on her cigarette, leaning in the doorway, scratching herself, the newspaper trapped under her arm, her expression undergoing rapid changes as she frowned, grinned, gestured rapidly with her free hand, painting a gaudy picture of her crowded, difficult life, hinting continually at her desperate need for money, making Sandra feel like stripping herself and handing her everything she possessed, down to the last stitch of clothing. It was exhausting. She lay down on the bed while Amy talked, and fell asleep.

When she woke, it was dark. The cream room and the green curtains were unfamiliar. She heard voices outside: Amy's and another's which cut into Amy's chatter frequently, evenly, stopping the flow. She went outside.

They were sitting at the dining table. They both turned to look at her. The resemblance between them made them seem like sisters.

"Look the girl from Berbice," Amy declared, pointing.

"Hello Sandra." This was Daphne. She was taller than Amy, better dressed, but her face as lined, and she smoked too. She held out her hand, took Sandra's and beckoned her to a chair.

Four five-dollar bills lay on the table. Daphne turned to Amy, "Look, don' argue with me. Is twenty dollars, an' no more, dammit. Don't tell me I can't count."

"But mistress," Amy protested. "This is always happening you know. I tell you is an extra dollar. If I was union member..."

"You damn bareface tellin' me 'bout union. Look, go 'long you way."

Amy rose, looking miserable, swept the money up and stuffed it into her bosom. "We have to discuss this more, man Mistress."

Daphne waved her away and sighed, then turned away. "So, how?" she asked Sandra, smiling.

"Until," Amy said, leaving.

"You find your way here all right," Daphne commented, ignoring Amy.

"Yes, Mummy drew a map."

"Helen always was a Georgetown lady. Knows this place

61

still like the back of her hand. How Daddy?"

"Well, thanks."

"Last time I see you, you were a small girl, nine years old. You're a young woman now. You remember me from that time?"

"Yes, you had on a black dress, a straw hat..."

Daphne laughed. "Lord, all that you remember? I hear Ben wasn't happy to let you come."

"I didn't know..."

"Yes man, I hear he gave the same trouble with high school. That man, he left all his family in Georgetown and he stay behind God back in that broken-down place. I never understood Ben. He like a savage. Stubborn like a mule. I must be the only one bother to keep in touch with him."

Daphne's fingers trembled when she took the cigarette to her lips. She drew hungrily on it. Her fingers were stained with nicotine."

"Years pass and I in' see that man. He don't go anywhere?"

Sandra remembered the Christmas cards. "No, only to town to do some buying."

"I bet Helen runs the business. She always was the better business woman. If she had total control, you all would have been better off..."

"Daddy is all right."

Daphne looked surprised. "Oh, you defending Ben? I hope you don't take after him. He's not a good example. He don't know how to get by."

"He only wants contentment. Nothing wrong with that."

Daphne harumphed. "I don't share your attitude, my dear."

Sandra remembered Daphne's part in the drama around Ben's and Helen's meeting. His mother had gone to Georgetown to find a match for him. Friends pointed out Helen, and Sarah agreed to a meeting in Pheasant. Ben fell for Helen instantly, and the wedding was agreed on. Daphne was heartbroken. Ben was more than a cousin to her. She quarrelled with Ben for days

62

after Sarah and Helen returned to Georgetown. Things came to a head when she ripped up the photograph of Helen which Sarah left him. She claimed that Ben slapped her because of it. The two families became estranged and, eventually, Daphne and her parents moved to Georgetown.

Daphne looked at her watch. "Seven o'clock. You sleep long. You have to be at work at eight tomorrow. I must warn you about Amy. She is a t'iefing woman. Mind don't talk to her and let her get too big for her shoes. She will always try to get things off you. She is the biggest liar in this place. Anyway, you won't see her, with your working hours. She is one a' these poor people and her hand fast. I hope Helen tell you the circumstances you coming into - I is a busy woman. I don' be home much. So is a lonely house. If you make friends, make decent friends. Good night. I must go to bed.

Sandra lay awake for a long while. Daphne and Amy were unnerving, hard women. Daphne was better off, but they both seemed to enjoy the haggle over the money, as if it were a ritual they indulged in often. Helen had never mentioned that Daphne was hardly home, that her house was lonely, and it had not occurred to her to wonder what kind of life Daphne lived. In Pheasant it had seemed too remote. She fell asleep, and dreamt of Pheasant. She saw Laila in the kitchen, singing as she cooked; Jay and William playing in the yard; Ben and Helen in the shop; and Sarah was there too, as if she hadn't died, working in the garden. Then her dream telescoped and she saw the whole village at dawn, with the pale blue sky and wispy clouds like a dome over the scene, with the canefields lining the canals all around. It was already so far away, with nothing for comfort here and she knew she disliked Daphne.

In the morning, Daphne was gone. There was a note on the table, with two sets of keys: Daphne would be home at midnight, the keys were for the front and back doors, and the bicycle downstairs which Helen had asked Daphne to buy her; it was important to shut all the windows and doors before she went out, and before she went to bed.

She rode out on the bicycle to join the flow of traffic towards the centre of town. The cars and cycles converged at the traffic lights, then set off in directions outlining squares and corners. Georgetown was bigger than New Amsterdam, which used to be the business and trading centre of the colony, but like New Amsterdam the smell and sight of the slums were never far away, the underbelly which occasionally turned urban Guiana upside down and rained down anarchy. Regent Street was lined mostly by stores and small eating houses, but people also lived there, in flats and houses squeezed into the alleyways - schoolchildren could be seen leaving their homes there. Already, the tramps and beggars were out on the pavements, and porters were pushing their barrows along the sheltered pavements towards the wharves of Water Street. The pavements outside the restaurants were being hosed down. The smell of rotting fruit wafted from Bourda Market where dray carts and trucks were arriving from the country to deposit their goods. Buses and taxis were ferrying passengers to work, newspapers were being sold at the corner of Camp and Regent Streets.

Water Street and Main Streets were the real commercial heart of Georgetown, and clustered around them were the streets of Brickdam and Kingston which between them embraced the places which supported this commerce: government offices, the law courts and lawyers offices, the embassies, the British Council, the four exclusive schools mainly for the children of the elite, the Anglican Bishop's High School and Queen's College and the Roman Catholic St. Stanislaus and St.Rose's where poor boys and girls could and did get in.

The Daily Mail offices were in Kingston, near Water Street. Here the city noises melted to a vague din. The street was lined by cars.

The Daily Mail building was like a huge warehouse, open and squat. The corrugated zinc roof was a down-turned V, its sides rising widely to its apex. Indoors, fans hanging low from the rafters whirred overhead. Waist-high partitions broke up the open space in the middle of the building. Signs hung from low chains from the rafters over each segmented area, designating ACCOUNTS, REPORTERS, ADVERTISING, LIBRARY, RECEPTION, PHOTOGRAPHERS. At the back of the building, a wire-mesh screen separated the printing presses from the rest of the office. Three guardhouse-like rooms stood outside the open area, their doors labelled EDITOR, MANAGER and PERSONNEL MANAGER.

A thin, heavily made-up woman in a brown shirt and orange skirt, her hair piled high in elaborate curls, answered her knock on the editor's door. She took the editor's letter between her thin fingers full-stopped by long, red-painted nails, and read it.

"Please wait outside," she said. "I'll tell the editor you're here. Take a seat in the reporters' section please."

She sat at the desk labelled FEMALE REPORTER. It was an old, chipped and battered desk, the polish faded. A wire basket, stuffed with dusty files and loose pages, perched on the desk. The drawers were overstuffed too, so weighed down, they stuck at half-shut, half-open angles.

Staff were still arriving: photographers came in with their cameras carried on straps round their necks and shoulders; the typists in the advertising and accounts section were uncovering their typewriters; the printing presses in the background were being worked; the messengers sat at the large, empty table in their section, talking and laughing. At the far left of the building, a sign, CANTEEN, hung over an open doorway, and women in white aprons and hats, like those worn by some servants who worked in the town homes in Berbice, passed in and out the doorway, carrying covered trays, baskets and basins. All the noises and movement in the building were taking shape as it filled up.

Four young men came to the reporters' section. Three murmured 'Morning', and one gave her a frank, questioning look. The tallest, thin, with a gentle expression, came to her.

"You must be the new female reporter," he said. "Sandra Yansen."

"Yes."

He offered his hand. "Welcome. My name is Paul Morgan. We're all trainee reporters. You're the latest addition. The older men in charge here. We take orders. Come and meet the fellows."

"Paul, you being the gentleman as usual?" The first reporter taunted him. He was squat and muscular, with a round, serious face, a pugnacious set to his lips, large ears, and a thick nest of hair.

"Stanley Bradley, Sandra Yansen," Paul Morgan introduced them.

Bradley said, "Don't let Paul mislead you. This place is a madhouse." He spoke evenly, lacing his voice with mockery.

"Don't take on Bradley," Morgan advised, and led her away.

"Owen Stamp, Sandra Yansen." Stamp was tall and broad-shouldered. His shirt was unbuttoned to expose his pale, bony chest where a heart-shaped medallion hung from a gold chain round his neck. He wore thick spectacles, and a cigarette smoked between his full lips. He shook her hand limply.

Bradley called out, "Stamp is the brightest here. Got an A at 'O' levels in Latin. Our St. Stanislaus boy from the slums, red boy."

Stamp waved dismissively at Bradley. "Any help you need, let me know," he said.

Bradley added, "Watch him, Miss Yansen. He's a sweet man. All the women like him - and men." Bradley howled with mirth.

Morgan said, "Come and meet a better species of humanity, Mark Lewis. Mark, this is Sandra, Sandra Yansen."

Lewis rose to shake her hand, smiled and said, "Welcome. We keep losing female reporters. I hope you stay." He drew a chair near the desk, and gestured, inviting her to sit.

Morgan sat on Lewis's desk and said, "Why you want to leave a nice place like Berbice and come and work in a hellhole like this?"

"Ah, Paul," Lewis said, "don' put off Sandra. Don' listen to

Paul, he's a pessimist." He turned to her. "Your first job?"
"Yes."

Lewis shrugged nonchalantly. His desk was tidy and clean, with a fresh sheet of blotting paper in the pad. Unlike Bradley's and Stamp's, but like Morgan's, his hair was neatly cut and combed round his head. "If you keep your mind on the work it's all right, and ignore the distractions. A lot depend on the Big Chief, the editor..." he said.

Morgan cut in, "The man is a tyrant. He tells you exactly what you must write. You ever hear about censorship? This is it, par excellence..."

Lewis looked pained. "Take it easy Paul. There's censorship and censorship. The editor got a thing about politics..."

Morgan guffawed, "A thing! Understatement of the year. The man is a politician."

She felt out of it. First Bradley's insulting manner, now this heated disagreement. She listened to them: Lewis was cautious, Morgan smouldering with outrage about their situation. Morgan thought they had no freedom of speech. Lewis did not like getting involved in politics. Stamp had nothing to say. Bradley was just unpleasant.

"Look, the Ton Ton Macoute comin'," Morgan declared. "The so-called editor."

Morgan hopped off the desk and left them. The editor wore dark glasses, a cream shirt and black trousers. His upper lip was deformed by a deep scar.

"Miss Yansen, welcome," he said. "I am very busy this morning, and can't stop to chat. I've left orders with my secretary to describe the terms of your employment. You've met the ah...staff?" He surveyed the others. Bradley was watching them intently. "You'll spend the first few weeks in here, learning the ropes, with one or two varied assignments. Anything you write, show me first." He smiled wanly. "One point I must make. Our readers have been complaining about the poor quality of our writing. I'm sure that you, as a reader, may have observed instances where our reporters' English leaves much to be desired. Now, you have a good grade in English. I am expecting a lot from you. There is very little I can do about this state of affairs since I did not employ the present staff. Would you believe, one actually told me English was not his forte?" He glanced at Bradley, who was still watching them intently. "However," he continued, "you must do your best. I have certain reading material in the office which you may peruse. My secretary will fetch some out for you. You may spend your time today reading. You must keep up with your reading of *Time* and *Newsweek* magazines, which are provided free here. I've told the library to expect you, so feel free to wander in there and acquaint yourself with our past history and tradition. Now I must go."

Once the editor was out of sight, Morgan groaned loudly, "God give me strength! *Newsweek! Time Magazine!* American propaganda!"

Bradley snarled. "What else there is to read in this country? Is either American, British or Russian propaganda to choose from. To me there is no difference between the three."

"What Russian propaganda?" Sandra asked Bradley. "I never read any Russian propaganda."

"You hear it though, from Cheddi Jagan and his wife, them two communists. You come from coolie country. You support them?"

"Shut you mouth Bradley," Morgan warned.

Lewis joined in. "Yes, shut up Bradley. You really go too far sometimes."

Sandra ignored their chivalry. "Where you calling coolie country? Berbice?"

"Yes," Bradley snapped.

"Why you call it coolie country?"

"Because coolie people live there. Rich rice farmers."

"Well, you don't know what you talking about at all. Some of the poorest people in this country live where I come from and you should be ashamed of yourself calling them 'coolie'. That is the word the old slave masters use. It shouldn't make you proud to use it."

No one said anything and she sat at Lewis's desk. He was reading the newspaper, his expression cool and detached.

"What exactly d'you do?" she asked him.

He dropped his paper. "Transcribe things. I get to write the odd review here and there, of a film, a painting exhibition, a novel. I help read the proofs, and I help out in the library."

"What about outside reporting...?"

He shrugged, "Oh, the experienced chaps do that, the older reporters. We don't see a lot of them. They're out a lot. We're trainees you know."

"Well I better go and get those books from the editor's secretary."

The secretary gave her two books: *Essential Journalism* and *The Small Town Newspaper*. She spent half the morning reading these, until Lewis invited her to join them in the canteen.

The canteen was filled with staff. The tables were packed close together, and people jostled at the counter for coffee, soft drinks and cakes. Talk at the tables was loud and jocular: repartee flowing easily between the typists, waitresses, messengers, photographers and accounts staff. The reporters sat together.

Bradley asked her, "How you like it so far?"

"Too early to say," she replied.

"You know, all the female reporters ever do is cover beauty contests and fashions?" Bradley said.

Morgan said, "Bradley doing crime and sports you see, so he thinks that make him the cat's whiskers."

"What you do?" she asked Morgan.

"Courts. I get to see justice in action." He spoke sarcastically.

Bradley chuckled and pointed to Stamp. "And Stamp here is the editor pet. He does something called current affairs, which mean anything under the sun he feel like doing." He slapped Stamp's shoulder. "This Stamp so sweet, the editor give him everything he want. Sometimes I wonder what really going on between you two, Stamp."

Stamp was irritated. "Bradley shut up. You just

jealous."

"Is because you don' give a shit about what going on around you," Bradley retorted. "You only looking after you own skin..."

Stamp got up and left. Bradley turned to her and asked, "Which school you went to? Bishop's?"

"No," she replied. "What about you?"

Morgan chuckled, "We all went to schools where you come out with a chip on your shoulder, Queen's College and Saint Stanislaus. By the time those schools finished with you, you screwed up for life, especially if you were poor when you went there, like us. Nothing else is good enough for you after that."

Bradley cut in hotly, "Morgan, take you miserable self somewhere else."

Lewis sighed. "Christ, y'all shut up. You behaving like asses."

"Never mind, Lewis," Bradley taunted. "When communism come to the country, it won't matter which school anybody been to. They talking 'bout independence, and dropping large hints about getting rid of the 'shackles of colonialism'. That mean us, an anybody with a colonial education. Christ, imagine fifty years from now what kinda people will be living in this country if it turn communist? People who never read the books we read. Education will be pure propaganda and brainwashing of one sort or the other."

"All education is brainwashing," Lewis said, "if you look at it closely. It different in content only according to who dishing it up. In the end, is the youth being corrupted and used by mad, corrupted people of one mental set or another. But I don't intend to spend time worrying about it. I doing my own thing."

Bradley pointed to Lewis. "Lewis is a philosopher. The biggest cop out of all, hiding behind philosophy. Any Tom, Dick and Harry can be a philosopher. You only got to say so. You don't have to prove anything."

The argument between them was clearly an old, familiar one. They understood what it was about. It was about their education and what it had done and not done for them, but they spoke almost in code, a school code they were trapped in. Bradley called Lewis a philosopher but Lewis was not. Lewis was saying that he wanted to be an individual but it threatened the group too much for Bradley, who needed the group most of all, to acknowledge this fact, so Bradley gave him a role which in his mind fitted Lewis into the group, the role of thinker and philosopher.

Bradley had reminded her that she was an outsider, that she came from 'coolie country', the sugar plantations. It reminded her that although they were lost in their own city, they would never be as alienated from it as she was. When Bradley expressed his racial and political prejudice he did it casually, almost playfully, with no sense of offence, complacent in the Georgetown bias. Already, one of their number, Owen Stamp, had decided that his fortunes lay with the new Government, and it only made Bradley uneasy because it was so tempting for him to follow Stamp in that direction, Stamp to whom he was especially attached.

Now they began to gossip. Stamp and Bradley revealed all their envy in their gossip about the rich youths of Georgetown with whom they had gone to school at St. Stanislaus, rich boys who had now gone abroad or returned to their lives of privilege to help a parent run a prosperous business, while Bradley and Stamp were returned to their humble origins. They could not be part of the white and coloured professional and commercial middle class, although they themselves were coloured, but they retained a sense of the exclusiveness they had learnt at St. Stanislaus, they mimicked it and transposed it to lower class situations, like the newspaper office where they behaved like an elite. Their rebelliousness was expressed in an underworld romanticism (they spoke enthusiastically of Henry Miller and Jean Genet) which was both literary and political but only veiled very thinly the biases of St. Stanislaus. Now Stamp, most adept at intellectual and political slogans, saw his opportunity to join a new black elite. He could play black or white as he liked since he

71

was both. St. Stanislaus had given them a thirst for privilege and the new government provided an avenue to a new kind of privilege where their talent for slogans could be put to good use. The break from the old establishment to the new establishment was testing out the group. The previous government, Jagan's government as they called it, was too preoccupied with the old world, the past, with destroying the plantations and the poverty there, so Georgetown had overthrown it. There was no remorse here among them for that, except from Paul who had gone to Central High School and had not tasted power and privilege as Stamp, Bradley and Lewis had. The remorse they felt was the remorse of the individual for his lot and a desire to rise against the bad card fate had dealt them - a perverted individualism without a moral code to it, only revenge and opportunism.

When they returned to the reporters' section, Paul took up the editor's books and threw them into the wastepaper basket. He brought her Albert Camus's *The Stranger*, and said, "Read this instead."

"Why?" she asked.

"Because it about how not to be brainwashed."

She read the blurb. "It's about a murderer."

"It's about a human being who wants only to be left alone in a madhouse called life."

"Morgan, you're the most pessimistic person I ever met."

"Tell me what there is to be optimistic about?"

"Well, not much. But don't let it make you totally negative. Save something of yourself if you can."

"So you think I'm negative."

"This book looks so depressing."

This hurt his pride. He wanted her to share their romanticism. "All right, don' read it then."

"I will read it. I not afraid to read it. I read *The Plague* by Camus and I like his writing."

He laughed. "So you all have books in Berbice?"

"I went to Berbice High School, not your Queen's College or Bishop's High School, but quite elitist in its way. It's more like the school you went to, Central High School, fee-paying enough to be respectable but too new to be colonial, traditional."

He raised a warning finger at her. "You sound like a Marxist to me. Don't tell me you been reading all this Communist propaganda the last government brought into this country."

"I used to visit their bookshop in New Amsterdam. It made a good change. I thinking of going to the university."

"That is the place they called the 'Communist night school', you know that?"

"You really believe that? Some of the best articles I ever read in the papers were written by some of the staff there. But I suppose Bradley would say they come from 'coolie country' too."

"Bradley upset you?"

She shrugged. "He doesn't seem to care about much, except himself."

Paul tapped *The Stranger*, "Stanley is an existentialist."

She changed the subject, not wanting to contradict his view of Bradley. "You ever go to the Sunday lectures at the university?"

"I tell you, that is a Communist night school." He laughed playfully.

"There are other courses there apart from politics. Literature for one. I hear they are giving some talks on Caribbean writers, Mittelholzer to start with..."

"That fellow who write all that Kaywana trash?"

"He's written some good things..."

Paul turned up his nose. His one failing up to now was the power over him of the male camaraderie among them which Bradley inspired. It warped his ideas. He mistook Bradley's prejudices and inadequacy for romantic existentialism. Even European intellectual ideas, like European materialism, could symbolise a vague future here, a way out of the Guianese impasse. It could lift you out of squalor. It was not just their reading of the French existentialists which attached Paul to

73

Bradley, it was also the rudeness of being Guianese men together, the wrongness and the strongness of it. Bradley was the most macho of the men and his word was law among them. Bradley, who was the swarthy mulatto like Mittelholzer, spurned that author, so they did too. Bradley looked down on women, kept them in their place and they, a little shamefacedly, did so too. It was the most powerful bond among men, it cut across class. It would have united all of St. Stanislaus and so it was not to be undervalued. And it was Paul, the Central High school man, the co-ed school, whose conscience was least easy in the role of the macho, whose conscience was most easily touched by injustice, so it was he who defied Bradley and defended causes against Bradley most.

The reporters' section was deserted most of the day. The advertising section was busiest. The customers came and went in a steady flow there. The posting and adding machines and typewriters kept up a jarring rhythm, taking turns at threading the foreground activity of talk and movement, sometimes combining as a steady backdrop. It was clear the reporters' work was less routine. When they did come in, they stayed briefly, to type an article or see someone.

She spent the afternoon reading in the library: a narrow room lined with close shelves of bound newspapers and boxes of photographs. Just before four, the senior reporters came in, and the trainee reporters followed shortly after.

Clinton Persaud, the chief reporter, came to greet her. "I hope you like it here," he said, smiling. "You're the latest in a long line." He patted her shoulder reassuringly. "Hold fast girl, hold fast. This boat rocking bad," he said, provocative, paternal. "The editor has spoken with you?"

"Yes, briefly."

"He gave you any assignments?"

"No. He said I should read some books."

Persaud shook his head. "What is wrong with this man? He has you young people hanging about here like decoration. You saw the telex? I want you to do some transcribing from the CANA news for me. Awright? Don' bother with no books. The best way to learn is to do writing all the time. Get all the experience you can before this place shut down completely. It coming you know. Censorship on the way in this country." With that, he waved and left the office.

Bradley watched him go, and said sarcastically, "Another damn politician. He say the CIA infiltrating the country, and the first thing they going to do is control the newspapers."

Morgan defended Persaud. "Clinton in' no politician. He is the only one know anything about journalism in this place. If wasn't for him, this place would be a complete joke."

Stamp sucked his teeth. "The man is a troublemaker. I don't like this damn politics at all. I don't believe in politics. Why don't they leave this country in peace?"

"Sandra," Morgan called. "I taking you to a beauty contest tonight." He waved two tickets. "Your first assignment."

Bradley laughed loudly. "What I tell you. I bet is the editor's orders. Miss Yansen, you will find that with Persaud and the editor, you between the devil and the deep blue sea. The editor will be sending you to beauty contests and nurses graduations, foundation-laying ceremonies, and Persaud will be training you to do investigative reporting, getting you into this freedom of speech shit, as if there is such a thing..."

"Bradley, nobody ask you for an opinion. You too damn bombastic and arrogant."

All day, the zinc roof, heated to a pitch, sent heatwaves down into the office. The fans gave little relief. When the presses went into operation, the operators stripped to the waist. The women's make-up became pasty and they fanned themselves frequently and shook their blouses to ventilate themselves. The bare concrete flooring, cool in the morning, warmed quickly. The librarian, a plump friendly middle-aged woman, advised her to wear socks if she didn't want to catch cold from her feet upwards, with the floor cool one minute, hot the next.

At four-thirty, she joined the rush hour traffic moving to the centre, round the cenotaph. Drivers honked in irritation at cyclists and pedestrians when they passed too near. Motorcycles and bicycles swerved in and out the cars. She made a wrong turning, into Robb Street, where two cars had collided in front of the Metropole; their owners were near coming to blows, while the waiting queue outside the cinema looked on quietly. Drivers, caught in the jam which was building up slowly, left their cars and joined in the swearing and rage-letting between the two protagonists. A beggar leaned against the lamp post at the roadside and gave an eye-witness commentary on the accident, which he had observed from start to finish. A juke-box blared in the cake-shop opposite the cinema, and the youths dancing on the pavement joined their howls of mirth at the carry-on to the confusion. She stood in the crowd. Lewis sailed past nonchalantly on his bicycle, and Morgan followed a minute or two later. He spotted her in the crowd and beckoned to her, stopping at the roadside.

"Sandra, you crazy?" he asked her. "You see where this confusion happening? A party headquarters right near here. People only want an excuse like this to throw a bomb or start a riot."

"What about some on-the-spot reporting?" she suggested, joking.

Morgan gestured dismissively. "This is peanuts. We only report accidents when somebody get mash up. Human interest, the editor call it."

He cycled with her to Daphne's cottage. "I will call for you at eight o'clock," he said. "Look, when they start sending you alone on night assignments, make them pay for a taxi. They used to send all the others out on night assignments, and one or two get assaulted and leave the job."

"What? Assaulted?"

He gave her a cutting look. "I watching you good. You don' know what you let yourself in for coming to this place. Why you don' stay home?"

"You're a very gloomy fellow. Tell me something? What's going on in the office between Persaud and the editor?"

"You notice something?"

"Well, Persaud criticized the editor, and Bradley said he's a trouble-maker, and Stamp seem to go along with him, and you on Persaud side..."

Morgan harumphed. "Girl, this country is a strange place at the moment, you hear. All that trouble with the race riots we had last year in' died down yet you know. I think it only starting now in a way. People get so frighten, they now want to pretend politics don't exist. But trouble going to hit them hard one day and when they do make a choice, they going to have to make one in a hurry, and they bound to land their conscience in the wrong place..."

"You getting me more confused. Why you all don't talk facts?"

"Never mind. You just keep your ears and eyes open, and mind how you go."

"Lord, you make it sound like a spy film, full of intrigue, suspicion, as if nobody to be trusted."

"That is what Persaud worried about. He is a journalist first, a very professional journalist. He has no party loyalties. He thinks this country is heading for censorship, that's why he fights the editor. He suspect the editor trying to get rid of reporters who want to be critical, and filling the place up with people who don't care about politics. Look, I was never interested in politics when I went to that place, and I still not interested in politics. I tell myself I only want to be a reporter. But when I see the things the editor do, it make nonsense of the work, and I beginning to feel very strong about it."

"But what exactly is going on in the office? Whose side the editor is on? He is against Cheddi Jagan and a supporter of Forbes Burnham?"

"I never said so!"

"But it seem so."

"You be careful what you say. You see all that violence that went on in Georgetown? The people who cause it are in power now. I not ashamed to say I frighten of them **bad**"

"But people say is the British taking over again and they feel

77

more secure for it."

"That's because they stupid. What good the British ever did us?"

"They did Georgetown more good than Pheasant where I come from, where they still planters. We still live in nineteenth century conditions. Georgetown is a twentieth century colonial city. That's why they could believe in the British restoring democracy in 1965. So the editor must stand for British decency?

Morgan grunted. "Decency? That man? That Ton Ton?" He would say nothing more

He cycled off and she went indoors. Amy had been. Dinner was cooked and warm on the stove. The house was swept and dusted, the kitchen tidied. She showered, ate and sat down to read until Paul returned. She couldn't concentrate on *The Stranger*. Pat had said of her that she liked to piece things together, like a jigsaw, but now, nothing fitted. She longed for the days after school, being with Laila in the kitchen, with Pat and with T and Estelle. But even as she longed, her longing lacked conviction.   There was David at his Campbellville address; this small, silent cottage with its two hard women; the life of the Georgetown streets; the life of the newspaper office, with the editor, Persaud, Morgan, Bradley, Stamp and Lewis larger than life. Everything was yet without substance.

She was tired. She shut her eyes and tried to sleep. When she couldn't, she tried to write a letter to Ben and Helen. Nothing worked to calm her spirit. In the end, she sat and day-dreamed about home; trying to picture Jay and William running about in the village, playing cricket, Jay strumming his guitar and singing his favourite song, 'Rose', by Sparrow. She succeeded in losing herself in her day-dream, but it only disoriented her when she opened her eyes to find the house darkening. She felt restless. She wished Daphne would come home, that eight o'clock would hurry and come.

Paul called on the dot of eight. They cycled together to Thomas Street where the beauty contest was being staged. Paul was more cheerful, better company. He talked about himself more positively. He wrote poetry. A poem had come to him that afternoon, and that never failed to put him in good spirits. She asked what the poem was about. He wouldn't tell her.

"Ha girl, you don't know this place. It got people that does plagiarize other people poetry."

"Who would want to plagiarize poetry?"

He remained solemn, pedalling along, his back straight, his shirt billowing in the cool breeze, his head held high. "People very short of ideas in this country." He was silent for a moment, then asked, "Where you were when we had the race riots in '63?" he asked.

"At home, just finished school."

"People want to forget it. But I tell you, worse going to happen if we don't remember how Guianese massacre one another. I don' know why they don' have a Remembrance Day for all the people that get killed in Georgetown and Wismar, when we observe a minute silence. It would do this country good to remember. And they should insert a clause in the constitution to say that any form of racism or racial exclusiveness is a crime. Race will destroy this country."

They were the first to arrive. The school hall was empty, filled with rows of wooden seats. The curtained stage was decked out in coloured bulbs, potted plants and streamers. Music by Mantovani drifted through the building. The audience began to arrive. They sat in the back row. Paul pointed out public figures: 'official artists', 'John Citizens', 'Ton Ton Macoutes' and graded others along a sliding scale of the 'upper echelons' of Georgetown society.

"Show me one person you like here," she said.

"How you could respect anybody who accept authority that is sham?"

79

The contest began. She had been given a list of the names of the contestants with their 'vital statistics', the dimensions of their bust, waist and hips, their occupations and hobbies. The audience applauded politely all the while. Paul fell asleep and half asleep with boredom herself, she forced herself to make notes

When she got in, Daphne was still out. She forced herself to write her report. Then she forced herself to write Ben and Helen an optimistic letter, and decided she would call David tomorrow. Daphne still had not returned when she turned off the lights and went to bed.

In the morning, she took her article to the editor's office.
"The editor wants to speak with you," his secretary said.
"Ah, Miss Yansen, come in," he greeted her. "Sit down."
He took a long time to read the article. He put it aside when he finished, saying, "This is very good. I don't need to edit it. Only the best articles need no editing. I pride myself on having work I don't have to edit you know." He didn't look up when he spoke. "There is a matter I wish to speak with you about, concerning working conditions in the office. I expect in time you will become familiar with my way of doing things. Now I will speak honestly." It was impossible to read him. His eyes were blanked off by the black sunglasses. He swivelled his head slowly, from left to right, directing his attention leisurely from one point of the surface of the desk to another. He spoke slowly, impeccably, for effect. "There are certain troublesome elements at work among the reporters. I won't beat about the bush. Clinton Persaud is the chief bottle washer. Now, two things. One, I am in authority here, not Persaud. Get that clear. You take all your orders from me. Secondly, you may hear talk of a strike or walk-off among the staff. I wish you to ignore it. These matters don't concern you or I or people wishing to work, achieve and contribute to progress in this country. Do you understand me? That

80

will be all, Miss Yansen." He turned to his filing tray and reached for a file.

She sat hypnotised in the chair. He put fear into her. She left the office. He was still absorbed in the file. Stunned, she found her way to her desk, seeing the others, but not listening to them. Her mind cleared slowly.

The senior reporters as well as the trainees sat together at a desk, locked in an intense discussion. Paul came to her desk.

"Listen," he said. "Trouble brewing up today. We going on strike. The editor fired Persaud this morning." He walked towards the printing presses, and called to the men there, "Right fellas! Everybody out. Showdown come!"

"Get out the placards!" Someone shouted. "He fire Persaud!"

The typists, clerks, waitresses, messengers and operators congregated in the reporters' section. Persaud stood on a desk, and raised his hand for silence. When he had their attention he took an envelope from his pocket, drew out a letter and waved it to them.

"Look Comrades, the dismissal come. We know it was always coming. They try all kind of pressure. Try to prevent me coming back into the country when I went on holiday to Trinidad. Threaten to kidnap me and my family, harass me one way and another, like witholding me salary, refuse to print me articles. You all know very well I am affiliated to no party. I am a journalist first and foremost and I believe in the precious right to freedom of speech. It is one of the most valuable assets in a country like ours. Whoever in power, the people have to make sure of one thing: that they have the right to criticize, to disagree and make their needs and demands known, I repeat, of any government. They try to spread the rumour I am now a party man. You all know me long. You know I only put the truth first. I have had to take a stand I never dream I would have to take in this country, a stand against censorship. There is a dangerous move to control the newspapers in this country, by one means and another. I am not making a stand against one party in favour of another. I am making a stand against the coming of censorship to this country. I am taking a journalist's stand! I am being dismissed for practising what the man who wrote this letter called 'political activism'. I don't have to tell you which person in this office is a 'political activist'. He is so barefaced, he doesn't even trouble to hide it. I thank you all for coming out on strike to protest my dismissal. I don't know if it will get me back my job, but I thank you all."

Loud cheers went up from the crowd. The placards were held up: 'Reinstate Persaud' each proclaimed. The staff moved as one towards the exit. The editor's door remained closed. The advertising manager came to his door and shook his head disapprovingly.

She took up her handbag and followed them. Outdoors, they formed two files and walked up and down along the street. She joined Bradley, Stamp and Lewis where they stood, looking on.

Bradley said, "You choose a hell of a time to come and work with the Mail. We might all be out of work. I don' think the editor care one black cent about all this."

Stamp sucked his teeth. "These people stupid to risk their job just for Persaud. What he going to give them back in return?"

Bradley rounded on Stamp. "Stamp, you know what you are? A prostitute. You only understand buying and selling favours between people. Why you don' go inside and ask the editor for Persaud job?"

Lewis drew her aside. "Come, let's go 'way from here. A lot of trouble going to happen here today. I think you should go home."

"What sorta trouble?"

"Policeman, riot squad. It happened once before. People got hurt. Look girl, I live through one race riot in this country. I not able to watch more violence. You better go home."

She rode off with Lewis. Paul and Clinton Persaud were standing under a tree with a group of printing press operators and typists. Paul waved as they went by.

She parted company with Lewis outside Bookers, parked

her bicycle on a stack outside the supermarket, and walked into the store, towards the cloth department. She had noticed the colourful bolts of cloth in the windows, riding past Bookers, and thought Helen would be pleased if she sent her a few yards of something. The store was a huge, well-lit place, teeming with smartly dressed men and women, the women and shopgirls expertly made up, scent wafting off them when she passed near. She fingered the transparent chiffons and sturdy linens, her mind on the Mail, what Lewis had said about the threat of violence, and trying to picture Helen in a dress made of any one of the materials spread out along the counters. Suppose she did lose her job, she worried. She would have to return to Pheasant.

The troubles at the Mail roused a string of recollections. When there had been one national, united party, the People's Progressive Party, it was an euphoric, joyful time. It was liberation politics. People in Pheasant were united racially in support of the party because it signified for them the end of the rule of the plantation in their lives - that was the meaning of those early days of national politics and it was an extraordinary time which she would never forget because it was the first time Pheasant had glimpsed a real future that they wanted instead of inventing fantasy futures, impossible futures for their children. But the racial split in the party baffled them and they had lost their way since and become sceptical about politics, reading the intrigues in the newspapers just for the sensationalism, the lewd entertainment. Once the party became divided against itself and lost its united anti-colonial stance, there was nothing in politics for Pheasant, unlike the Corentyne where there were wealthy local businessmen with a vested interest in the ups and downs of Georgetown politics.

But the tragedies which began in 1961 sent shock waves through Pheasant: the 1963 race riots, the Wismar atrocities, political intrigue between the political parties, labour unrest on the sugar estates and the return of the British to resolve the political situation. The impact of all these things came at several removes to Pheasant, as news over the radio and in the

83

newspaper or rumour and hearsay. One thing did affect them directly, the arrival of some of the Wismar refugees in Berbice. She was at school then. At recess one day, a truck brought the refugees to the Lutheran Hall near the school. Before that, the newspapers had carried explicit news and photographs about the atrocities which took place: women raped and murdered, including pregnant women whose wombs were disgorged of foetuses which were flung into Wismar River. It was said that the river was strewn with bodies and dismembered limbs; men and boys were castrated; even the aged were not spared. The newspaper spoke of genocide and decimation of the East Indian race at Wismar. That day at school, the boys and girls had stood around the truck, watching the refugees disembark. They included men and women, children and babies, all dressed in clothing donated by the hospitals: starched and unironed loose fitting aprons tied round the waist. They had looked lost, distracted and dazed, not seeming to see the inquisitive schoolchildren.

Just before the race riots, when there was sporadic violence along the East Coast, the students from those villages brought rumour of atrocities: beheadings and gang beatings between the races. And in the middle of the English Language G.C.E. 'O' level exams, some policemen had come to take away Joe Beharry on a charge of gang murder. They learnt later that Joe was in jail, and Myrna Chandler had gone to the prison to invigilate his Latin examination. Myrna was so deeply affected by his situation, she made a long speech next day after prayers in the auditorium about the danger of political involvement. She spoke, like the romantic Guianese intellectual she was, of the fragility of life and the necessity for belief in Truth, Beauty and Reason, quoting Plato and Aristotle.

These traumas depressed the people in Pheasant and they preferred to forget it as quickly as possible. They made much of the drama of elections, as much as the men made drama of test matches in England and Australia, staying up all night to listen to radio commentaries, speculating wildly about winners and losers. The outbreaks of labour unrest on the estate held the same appeal. The villagers would support the leaders who stirred up action against the overseers, until loss of life and limb was threatened, or someone indeed was killed, then things would calm again, until the next confrontation.

These events had a way of telescoping: expanding and contracting in significance, like the images on the cinema screen when the projector went mad, the focus blurring, rocking, blanking out, flickering; while the audience flew into rages or sucked their teeth in annoyance at what seemed a deliberate subverting of their fantasies. Behind the real life dramas lay unreliable projectionists. Just as the villagers walked out of the cinema when the film failed, they switched off these things from their memories. They were bad memories: the failure of unity between the leaders, the long strike when they came nearest starvation, Wismar, the riots, the betrayals by the British Government: all blurred into one abstraction of injustice of which they were the living proof and victims.

For the young, it was left to school to provide focus, so they learnt their Latin, English grammar and history, French and science, and dreamed of a bright future of respectability and material well-being such as Bookers Stores symbolized.

Sandra was paying the cashier for four yards of green linen when she felt a hand on her shoulder. She turned to face David Petrie.

"Hello," he said. He was looking immaculate as ever, dressed in a white long-sleeved shirt and green tie with a gold clip, and black trousers. "I've been waiting for you to telephone, as you promised."

"Give me a chance. Just two days passed since I arrive."

"Everything all right?"

"There's a strike at the Mail."

He sighed and shook his head. "These people don't know when they have it good. They have something better to do than work?" He took her arm. "Come to the snack bar. Let's have a drink."

The waitresses at the snack bar called to him, "Hello, Mr. Petrie," and served him quickly.

"I work near here, with the auditors, Fitzpatricks," he informed her.

He was a stranger all over again. She couldn't think what to say to him. The waitresses, looking hot and harassed in their thick white cotton uniforms, shoved plates of sandwiches, rich cake and patties across the counter as they rushed to and from the concealed kitchen. The snack bar was filling up with customers. The stools were taken, but people jammed themselves between each other and clamoured for service or simply waited stoically. The fans behind the counter rotated steadily, doing little to clear the heat and closeness.

"This means you have nothing to do now?" he asked.

"It seems so. It depend what happens. Whatever, things look not so good." She shrugged. "I should try and look on the bright side."

"That newspaper is a hothouse right now. That fellow Persaud is a hothead, a Communist. They should get rid of him."

"That's what happened this morning. The editor sacked him. The staff are on strike to pressure the editor and manager into reinstating him."

"They've had some trouble there before. The riot squad came out, and one or two bones were broken from what I hear. You don' want to work in place like that, man. Why not apply for another job. Try my place. I can pull a few strings." He hopped off the stool. "I have to go now. I have a meeting. I will come and see you this afternoon." With a wave of his hand he turned and left.

Regent Street was just as it was the afternoon she arrived from Pheasant: half-awake, half-asleep in the heat. These two days had been as eventful and full as they had been dull and lethargic: from the clashes in the office to the vacuum of Daphne's cottage, from the trivia of the beauty contest to the drama of the strike.

She heard the news on the five o'clock current affairs radio programme: the Riot Squad had come out at the Daily Mail; Clinton Persaud had been arrested, with a few others, charged with disturbing the peace.

Daphne came in while she was listening. "Is time they get rid of that damn Communist! I hope they chuck him in jail and keep him there. They should send him to Siberia."

Sandra told Daphne about David Petrie, and asked if she would mind him visiting.

Daphne looked at her with new eyes. "Here only two days and have a boyfriend already?" There was a hint of disapproval in her voice, doubt in her expression.

She explained how she met David.

"Well," Daphne said, "if Ben and Helen know about it, I suppose it OK, but I hope he's decent. I am a respectable woman. As long as you don't do anything you shouldn't do, and you let me know how you coming and going."

David came at seven. Daphne's face softened and she smiled like a schoolgirl when she saw him. He shook her hand, and said, "Pleased to meet you, Miss Yansen." Daphne offered him a whisky. She brought Sandra a soft drink, and the same for herself. Then she sat with them and held him in conversation, questioning him about his background and connections in Trinidad and in Georgetown. David warmed to the interrogation. Breezily he supplied all the impressive facts: his parents were both prominent Trinidadian lawyers; they were an old, established Trinidadian family boasting a long line of medical and legal achievements; his older brother was a doctor and his sister was a law student in London. Daphne asked him why he had not done law or medicine. He replied that he was the dunce and black sheep of the family. Daphne consoled him that being an accountant was as good as anything else; there was as much money to be made there, if not more. Then they both began to drop the names of all the respectable Georgetown people they knew: a magistrate here, a bank manager there; and if they had not met some, they knew people who knew of them.

Sandra had sat in on boasting orgies before, but none so totally bolstered by complacency. Josephine used to boast out of fear of inferiority, others to assert themselves, but Daphne and David basked luxuriantly in their own infinite self-regard, as if nothing ever troubled or worried them, or ever could, feeding each other generously with praise and approval, gesturing in a parody of graciousness, as they conjured the worth of such and such a thing, or this and that person.

He was a chameleon: withdrawn and supercilious the first time; crude and offensive when he was irritated; reflective and philosophic near the river in Forest when the dark covered him; gallant at the snack bar and with her family; but now, his posturing with Daphne laid the ghosts of his other selves. It was all imposture. He changed for each occasion and circumstance.

Eventually, Daphne rose, saying with a giggle, "I must leave you young people to chat now."

When Daphne disappeared into her room, he sighed and stretched, shook his legs and turned to grin at her, shaking off one skin, about to put on another. "You heard the news about Persaud on the radio?" he asked. "It mean you can go to work tomorrow. You glad?"

"I will go in tomorrow and see what's going on. Perhaps the strike will go on."

He gestured dismissively. "No man. Persaud gone. There will be peace now. The people want their money. You know how it is. A little excitement and then things calm down. So it go."

When he left, she sat near the window and watched the cars, cyclists and pedestrians go by in an intermittent stream. The oleander trees provided a screen between the front yard and the street. The cottage was set back a good way in the large yard, so there was privacy from the street. For the first time, she was attacked by severe homesickness, and doubted herself completely. She did not belong in Georgetown. It was not enough that Helen and Sarah came from Georgetown. That gave her no right to be here. Any confidence that she had brought with her had gone and the loss swathed her until she rose and went to her room. She had to take each day as it came, for the time being, cope with routine and lethargy by setting herself tasks to do, and hope the unexpected did not happen.

In the morning, Daphne was gone by seven, and she set out more purposefully this time. The office was filling up when she arrived. Bradley, Stamp, Paul and Lewis were there.

"You hear the news?" Paul asked her.

"About Persaud? Yes."

"Not just that. We're in charge here. All the senior reporters hand in their resignation. The editor in control of us now. We take orders from him. The whole paper going to change. Wait and see, pure propaganda. All part of the new government."

The editor came round to the reporters' section. "Please gather round," he said, perching on a desk. He was carrying a large file, which he opened and studied thoughtfully, frowning. "I have your details here." He spoke to them as one. The movement of his hands, as he turned the pages, was elegant, economic. He wasted no look, no gesture, no word. He raised his head slowly, and directed his look to Stamp.

"Mr. Owen Stamp?" It was not that he was not sure who Stamp was. He did not suffer from uncertainty. He was more asking Stamp whether or not he, Stamp, was sure of his own identity; this was the implication his ironic tone carried. "Aha, what have we here?" He read along the page, nodding. He murmured, "I have been studying these records closely, as I did not take any of you on, apart from Miss Yansen. Now Stamp, from what I see here, I believe we may accord you the privilege of having a free hand at political matters. I think that would be right." He raised his head and regarded Stamp from behind his dark glasses. "Are you interested in politics, Stamp?"

Stamp was wearing dark glasses this morning. Unlike the editor, he did not know how to use them to create an expressionless mask. A grin broke out across Stamp's face. "As a matter of fact, yes," Stamp replied.

The editor looked down at the file again. He harumphed, and said nothing. Paul shuffled his legs restlessly. "As far as I am concerned, Stamp, political matters are top priority, the most important task of a newspaper, to let the public know what is being achieved in the sphere of ideas. I will speak to you therefore in greater detail as time goes on. All right?"

"Yes Sir," Stamp replied.

"The Ministry of Information is becoming a far more efficient place, and we can rely upon them for fact sheets which update our information, so bear that in mind, Mr. Stamp, and remember the Ministry of Information as an important source for your material."

Stamp nodded. The editor drew a deep breath and turned a page. "Now what have we next? A Mr. Stanley Bradley."

Bradley stiffened in his chair, and stared insolently at the editor. "The very same," Bradley returned.

The editor's head jerked up and a look of displeasure crossed his face. "You, Bradley, handle sports and help with proofreading," he announced abruptly. Bradley smirked. The editor turned another page. "Mr. Mark Lewis is next." Lewis sat at his desk, his legs crossed, looking worried. "Mr. Lewis, I see you have a penchant for the arts. Very well, you may have a free hand at that and do whatever pleases you in that area, but I am going to come to the matter of editorial policy by and by, and we will raise the arts again. But since that is not a full time preoccupation, I wish you to keep yourself free for varied assignments."

The editor looked up and regarded them, one after the other. "Now this is the key note: varied assignments. Apart from Stamp's task, we will not have specialisation in the office. And apart from Bradley's, of course. Miss Yansen, Mr. Morgan and Mr. Lewis must be at the ready to tackle varied assignments: crime, road accidents, the law courts, human interest stories, and the varied social matters that concern us. I will be directing these assignations very closely, until I am convinced you are experienced enough to follow your nose in certain areas. Our senior reporters are no longer with us." He turned down his lips in an expression of distaste. "In some ways, that is a blessing, in others, not..."

Paul cut into the editor, "It seem to me, Sir, that you will be writing the whole newspaper yourself."

The editor's mask crumbled and a look of extreme annoyance twisted his features. "I did not ask for your opinion, Mr. Morgan. You are not being paid to give me advice..."

"Wasn't giving advice," Paul retorted. Only stating what seem to be a fact."

Paul stood tall, thin, defiant, cool, a disdainful look on his face. All around them, the life of the office went on. Outside the canteen, the waitress was hanging up a sign with the day's menu; the operators were cleaning the printing presses; the messengers were fetching in the latest delivery of parcels. The editor struggled to regain his composure.

The editor said, "Leave me to decide the facts, Mr. Morgan."

"Facts can become very controversial when only one person stating them, and denying what other people think to be facts."

The editor nodded slowly. "I see what happening, Morgan. You wish to step into Persaud's shoes. You are a very ambitious young man. But if you're patient, your ambition will be rewarded." He looked at the file. "I think you should deal with crime, Mr. Morgan, and cover the civic ceremonies and official happenings." He looked up again. "But as I said, all this is flexible. Now, Miss Yansen, I can't be everywhere all at once. There is this very important matter of the Commission of Enquiry at the Red House, about this shooting at La Repentir sugar estate. I want you to go along and cover that. Generally, I want you to keep an eye on education, though that will overlap with political matters. You see, we are in a country where these things overlap very strongly. The books on journalism will tell you otherwise, that these things belong in different compartments. But in a pioneering country like ours, where the shape of things to come must yet emerge, we have to keep our imagination and thinking open..."

"...to corruption..." Bradley muttered, but the editor was outside hearing range.

The editor shut the file and took his weight off the desk. "That will be all today." His purpose had left him. "Collect your press cards from my secretary, and your assignments for today." He turned and made his way to his office.

They avoided each other's eyes, embarrassed and silent. Lewis did not linger, he went straight to the secretary for his orders. Stamp quickly followed him. Paul paced the section moodily. Bradley folded his arms and rocked back and forth in his chair, watching Paul cynically.

"Relax, Morgan," Bradley said.

Paul brushed his words away. "Shut up Bradley. Leave me alone."

Bradley turned to her. "Miss Yansen, you looking thoughtful. Well, the way to promotion open to us, if we do the right things."

Paul shook his head. "I don' like this set-up. I don' like it at all."

Bradley sighed. "Morgan, stop behaving like some statesman."

The editor's secretary came to the section. She handed them each a press card, and a memorandum each from the editor.

"Miss Singh, what you think about what happened to Persaud?" Bradley asked the secretary. She was as immaculately made-up and efficient as ever. She handed Bradley his press card and memorandum, and took her time replying to his question.

"What I think? Boy Bradley, I am a small fish in a big ocean, a small, small fish. You hear?"

"Ah," Bradley drawled, dismissive. "You know all the behind-the-scene-moves that went to get rid of Persaud. Tell we who involve..."

Miss Singh put her hands on her hips and stood over Bradley assertively. "Bradley, look me good. I been working in this place longer than you, but I know less than you. Don't play big man with me. I don't know anything, you hear? The editor has his own private telephone, with his own private connections. If you want to know something none of us know, you go and ask him yourself." She swung on her high heels, and returned to her office.

The editor's memorandum directed Sandra to attend the Inquiry with Paul. Paul's memorandum echoed the instruction.

"Why two of us?" Paul queried.

She hazarded a guess, "Maybe he thinks I don't have enough experience."

Paul warned, "Don't start providing excuses for the editor." He turned to Bradley who was preparing to leave. "Bradley, why you think the editor sending me with Sandra?"

Bradley shook his head and smirked cynically, "Maybe he's putting you out of action, Paul, and using the lady you like so much to do it."

If Paul had been hit over the head with a hammer, the shock could not have seemed greater. A chill passed through her. She turned on Bradley: "Bradley, if it's a joke you're making, it's a serious joke."

Casually Bradley left the section. She watched him go, with his leaping, springy walk. She turned to Paul. "Bradley don't like women."

Paul sat down. "I not coming with you. You go alone."

"Why?"

Paul shook his head. "I don't like this. I don't like it at all. I wondering, if the editor want to get rid of me, just how would he go about it." He looked at her. "You see what happened yesterday? That was how the editor planned it. He knew that if he dismissed Persaud, everybody would go on strike, and I believe he arranged with the powers that be for the riot squad to come and take him to jail. Once that happen, what we could do?"

She sat with him. "You're sure?"

He shook his head. "You can't be sure of anything anymore. Guys like the editor can do what they like. How they do it is just academic. You realize that make us so-called journalists redun-

93

dant? We don't know a shit who pulling what strings. All we know is somebody get frame-up and taken away." He gestured expansively round the office. "And look at yesterday's militants. Life back to normal. Only, I know it very well not normal. Girl, I tell you, this country under siege, but people don't know it. They won't know it till it hit them in the face. Give them ten, twenty years and see. I find the whole damn thing so soul-destroying, to sit here and stew and know you stewing and can't do a thing about it. Is pure impotence. These barefaced scamps! What happening now, 1965, is nothing compared to what going come later."

"Come, let's go to the Inquiry."

At Red House, they showed their press cards to the policeman at the gate. He was wearing a gun on his hip.

"You notice the gun?" Paul asked. "Policeman never wear gun in this country. You see what things getting to?"

They waited outside. When the cars began to arrive, Paul pointed out the lawyers on both sides, for the police, and for the relatives of the dead man. Reporters from the rival newspapers arrived next, followed by two carloads of policemen. Two police superintendents arrived in a chauffeur-driven car. A barefooted band of men and women came through the gates. Paul thought they were probably the dead man's relatives. The magistrate arrived last, chauffeur-driven, dressed in a black suit.

Indoors, they were directed to the press section. The barefooted group sat at the back of the room. The lawyers were spread out in a row before the magistrate's podium. The superintendents sat behind the lawyers, and the policemen, eight in all, sat behind the superintendent.

A door opened behind the podium, and two members of the riot squad entered. They wore their helmets, ammunition belts, heavy boots, and carried a rifle each. They took up positions on either side of the open doorway. One of the barefooted women began to weep into a hankerchief. The superintendents turned and signalled the group to calm her. The magistrate, an Indian, arrived in a flurry, stamping his feet, a pile of large books on his

94

left arm, a white wig in his right hand, his gown flowing behind him. His clerk followed on his heels.

"Somebody put on the fan," he demanded.

One of the superintendents hastened to obey. "It not working, Sir," the superintendent apologised.

The magistrate snapped, "Well fix it, man, fix it. They want me to boil to death?" He put on his wig and sat down. He turned to one of the riot squad men. "You, fella! Go bring me a jug a' water, and don' fo'get the glass." The riot squad man leaned his rifle against the wall and went throught the door. The superintendent was still struggling with the fan. One of the lawyers came forward to help. They laughed and joked over their task.

One of the policemen got up, and called to the superintendent, "Sir, I can fix fans."

The superintendent retorted, "How come you can fix fans and you can' use a gun?" He turned to the reporters, "He is the one charge with the shooting, you know." Everybody burst out laughing, including the barefooted group at the back of the room. One man in the group called out:

"He was always stupidy. I been to school with him on the West Bank."

"Write that down," the magistrate told his clerk. "That is important evidence."

The lawyers laughed loudly, and teased the young policeman as he made his way to the fan. He smiled back, sheepish.

Everyone became serious when the magistrate rapped on the podium and declared the Inquiry open. Rapidly he set out the cause for the Inquiry, the case for investigation, and proceeded to call the first witness. The superintendents took their turn in the witness stand. The lawyers did not cross-examine them, only the magistrate. He reeled off his questions from a sheet of paper, and the superintendents answered rapidly and efficiently.

Paul whispered, "This is one of these prejudged cases. You can usually tell. The magistrate is a lawyer, judge and jury all in one. The lawyers just decorations."

If Paul was right, the policemen had not learnt their lines well, especially the young policeman. He shook with nerves. He frequently asked the magistrate to repeat the questions.

"What happen?" the magistrate snapped. "You don't understand proper English?"

The policeman became flustered. He tried to speak 'proper English' as the magistrate ordered him to do. His discomfort increased. The situation deteriorated into more laughter and teasing at his expense. He became dumb with embarrassment and the magistrate dismissed him contemptuously from the witness stand.

At midday they returned to the Daily Mail. They rode along without speaking. Paul, already depressed by yesterday's events, the editor that morning and now the Inquiry, was sunk in his own thoughts.

Bradley, Stamp and Lewis were at lunch in the canteen.

"Listen," Bradley announced, "the editor doing exactly what you say he would do, Paul. The man writing the whole of the newspaper by himself, using a lotta foreign news coming through the telex, and," he pointed to Stamp, "propaganda Stamp collect from various government offices this morning, and my sports pieces."

Stamp was irritated. "Bradley, all editors edit. You don't know that? You making mischief. You all getting paranoid. Is Persaud make you all so."

Bradley shot back, "Stamp, you quickly turning into his right hand man. You don't see the man is phrasing everything carefully to make the paper eulogistic. Not a trace of individualism must appear in the printed word. You all go and read the material he sent for proofs. What I am talking about is voice, you hear, voice. Is not what is written, but how it is written, where the voice coming from. Boy, everything sound packaged, whatever you read, from the editorial to the sports page. I tell you, this thing is insidious. People think because they getting newspaper, there's no censorship. The man is doing it very subtly. He working for somebody."

Stamp grinned and jabbed a thumb at Bradley. "You love a drama, Bradley. Somebody just got to shout 'Wolf' and you running along."

Sandra said, "The Inquiry was a farce this morning."

Stamp commented, "Wait, you too? I tell you, you all suddenly find yourself with responsibility and you can't handle it. You resort to fear, suspicion and superstition..."

Bradley slapped Stamp on the shoulder. "You hear the editor's hack? He is the editor mouthpiece already. The editor plant a spy among us. Be careful what you say. Sandra, you just make your grave with what you say there. Don't criticize the judiciary. It will go straight back."

Stamp ignored him. "Persaud make you all ambitious to become stars..."

She left them and went to her desk. A letter from Jay lay on top of the file of scripts, with a note from the editor: "Miss Yansen, please transcribe these." She opened Jay's letter: "Dear Sis," it began, "I hope Georgetown treating you good. The old lady ask me to write you. She is not feeling very well lately, and was in bed all day yesterday, suffering with pain. We had to take her to the doctor in town, and they say she need an operation in a week or two. Don't do anything like rushing home. I will write again and let you know how things are going. Everything is under control here. Zena and Nurse helping to look after her and run things here. Your loving brother, Jay."

The building was deserted. The talk and laughter in the canteen echoed round the empty spaces. The airlessness seemed to trap every sound, like dust, so each particle of talk or laughter, though it faded, hung like an invisible substance in the atmosphere.

She read the scripts. In all, it was a jumble of details: here, an outbreak of a new cattle disease in the Rupununi, the appointment of a senior civil servant in the Ministry of Home Affairs, the opening of a new boutique in Main Street, a pithy comment from the Mayor about juvenile delinquency, a case of food poisoning in Ituni.

She read Jay's letter again, and imagined the worst at home. Helen was a strong woman, and suffered little from serious illnesses. The odd headache or fever she quickly threw off. At the most, one day in bed sufficed to restore her strength. She would wait for more news from Jay.

Miss Singh called from the editor's office, "Miss Yansen, the editor wants an article about the Inquiry, in two days!"

She was at work on the transcriptions when the others returned to the section. Bradley commented, "Ah Miss Yansen, you are diligent!" His voice was edgy and sarcastic. A file of transcripts lay on each of their desks. Bradley sucked his teeth loudly when he read his and exclaimed, "Pure shit! "

"Pure shit it may be, Bradley," Stamp said, "but is work to be done. Come man."

While they worked, the telephone rang, the typewriters and adding machines kept up a rhythmic background noise and people shouted across the building. Stamp finished his transcriptions and took them to the editor's office.

"Miss Yansen," Stamp called, "the editor say he hope you make a start on the Inquiry article. He is depending on it."

Bradley was restless. He slapped a book on his desk, sucked his teeth loudly and declared, "Stamp, you in charge of us here?" He looked at the others. "Look, I want to know officially if Stamp in charge here!

They ignored him. He shouted to Lewis, "Ai Lewis, you got me fucking ruler?"

Lewis gave him a cutting look, then put down his head again.

"Ai you, black boy, Morgan," Bradley shouted. "You got me ruler?"

Paul replied, "Bradley, you call me 'black boy' again, and I will push your blasted face in fo' you."

Bradley rocked back and forth in his chair. He had no intention of doing any work. He went to the canteen, and returned with a bottle of beer. "I going read a book," he declared. He waved the book in the air. "Anybody read this? *Memoirs of a*

Dutiful Daughter by Simone de Beauvoir."

They ignored him. "Miss Yansen, you should read it," he suggested. "I am very interested in women, what make them tick."

She went to Paul. "Paul, the Inquiry: the editor want me to write it up." She put her notes on the desk. "I transcribed everything that went on."

Paul read them, laughing darkly. When he finished he handed it back. "You know what the magistrate's conclusions were? Death by misadventure. Everybody see when the superintendent tell the policemen to open fire. It was no damn misadventure. It was murder. You being asked to get involved in the cover-up. You know that?"

"Yes," she replied. "That is what worrying me. I know the editor just wants me to transcribe. Transcribe, transcribe, transcribe..."

"That's right. Cover-up, cover-up, cover-up."

"What to do?"

He shrugged, "I can't tell you what to do. I know what you're expected to do: just give a mechanical account of the Inquiry procedure, like you see in the trial reports."

"You were there. You noticed how the whole thing was manipulated."

"These courts like that. Pure comedy and farce. You see how the dead man relatives join in the joking too? Is they who suffer you know. No justice, no compensation. Country people stupid bad..."

"They were in the magistrate's hands. You can't say that."

He harumphed. "We can go on making excuses for them for ever. Persaud, I sorry he not here. He could help you out. He had a subtle way of handling these things. The reporters depended on him a lot. He was like our conscience in this place. He would let them print the cover-ups. But he used to write critical articles about the judiciary here and there, about the civil service and the Chamber of Commerce. That's why he got in trouble. That's why we here today, doing everything."

"Well, he's not here now."

"You're right he's not. I feel somebody should replace him. I was like a small boy depending on Persaud. But I think it becomes a burden to men of conscience, to have people depending on them to do all their thinking. Look where he is now - in jail. I feel I for one help to put him there. We free as birds, and Persaud roasting in jail."

"Don't talk stupidness. You didn't put Persaud in jail. Your mind jumping too far. Be realistic."

He gave her a cynical look. "You women don't understand these things."

"That's supposed to be my cross?"

"We all carrying a cross in this country, girl."

The editor had come to the reporters' section. He was standing outside the partition, arms akimbo, without his sunglasses, looking irritated. The flesh around his eyes was crinkled, and a darker hue than his face. His eyes were red, blood-shot. "Miss Yansen, Mr. Morgan, are you having a tea party?" he reproached them. He turned his look of irritation on Bradley. "Mr. Bradley, this is not a rum shop. Kindly take that beer bottle back to the canteen, and take your feet off the desk." He ambled up to Bradley's desk and lifted the book from his hands. "What are you reading?" He sucked his teeth and threw the book down on the desk. He turned to face the group. "Have you all finished your transcriptions?" They nodded, except Bradley who was glaring insolently at the editor. "Good, I will have them in my office by four. Now, look here, you will all have to stay on tonight. There isn't enough news for the paper tomorrow. We have to supplement with some foreign matters. Get busy round the telex and transcribe anything you think newsworthy. I want a steady flow of foreign transcriptions coming into my office. I think we had better leave that to Yansen, Lewis, Morgan and Bradley. Stamp, you and I will have to keep our interest in political matters." He turned to Stamp. "Did you meet those contacts in the Ministries this morning?"

"Yes Sir," Stamp replied. "They were helpful."

"I expect them to be," the editor returned. He rubbed his

eyes, drew his dark glasses from his pocket and put them on. "That will be all. Miss Yansen, please complete that Inquiry report and let me have it quickly. Then get on with the task I have outlined."

They worked until eight that night. The foreign news poured in, an endless flow from the machine. Bradley ripped the sheets savagely, and kept up an endless obscene chatter: "What the shit I care about the British Government stand on this or that, and fucking European shit, or space exploration in America or Russia?" But he sat down and transcribed. Lewis and Paul worked in stony silence. Stamp worked alone on politics, especially the talks in London about plans for independence, and had to go to the editor's office so frequently he eventually disappeared in there.

Bradley, Lewis and Morgan cycled her home, Bradley riding behind the group, singing at the top of his voice and, in between, shouting obscenities and taunts at various pedestrians, passing cyclists and cars.

Daphne was in, chain-smoking in the morris chair. "So late you come home?" she asked, frowning.

"There's a lot of work to do in the office."

"Make sure you get paid overtime for it. I know the editor. I will speak to him about it." "I didn't know you knew him."

"How else you think you get the job? I play poker with him."

Sandra sat down. Daphne was wearing her spectacles. Her wiry hair fell in loose crinkled strands from the untidy bun at her neck. The spectacles were connected by a thin chain round her neck. The cigarette was burnt down to the filter which, damp with saliva, stuck to her thin lower lip. She screwed up her eyes as she read, holding up the newspaper near her face.

"I thought I got the job on my own," she told Daphne.

Daphne glanced at her. "Things don't work out like that. When you applied for the job, Helen wrote and asked if I knew anybody who could make sure you got the job. You see, Helen

101

understand how things work here."

"But Mummy didn't tell me."

Daphne looked puzzled. "So what?" she boasted, "I work with a lawyer, and they tend to know everything and everybody. Naturally, Helen know I have contacts."

Through dinner, and her shower, uncomfortable resentment welled in her, that the last thread of connection between her will and her fate was cut through so casually. She took her notes about the Inquiry to the table. Daphne was still reading. Her presence distracted Sandra so much that she could not concentrate on the report. The smell of stale tobacco filled the cottage. Washed by the light orange haze of the bulbs, one over Daphne, one over the table, the old wooden walls of the cottage seemed a small, islanded enclosure of narrow comfort in a sea of life and darkness. Daphne basked in her comfort, shored up by acquaintances, money and the sureness of the directions she took when outside the cottage.

Life was crowded in the city streets. You moved in confined spaces. Ever since she had arrived, Daphne, Amy, the people at the Mail, in the stores and in the street, had begun to people the space of ignorance which she had brought with her from Pheasant. And everything they did and said entered the store of impressions she was creating. She thought of David when he came to Pheasant, how he had fought against what he had found there, adopting various stances which asserted his own familiar attitudes and habits. He had not come with the silence of his ignorance. His very body was like an object or a wall which he used to block off what he named uncivilized, empty, nothing, the words tumbling from his lips like bits of substance from his flesh. He quarrelled with what he found there. The substance of his thoughts was his own flesh itself, feeding and asserting itself. Only once had he let himself be ignorant, when they were near the river in Forest, and he had spoken of endless space, and his flesh seemed to fall from him like so many walls, leading him back down the corridors of his boyhood, buried deep in his unconscious. It made him uncomfortable. Quickly, he reclaimed flesh again, invoking the words 'control', 'confidence', 'advantages and disadvantages', 'challenge', 'competing', telling her that she would understand when she went to work.

Outside, it began to drizzle. The rain came down in spots on the window pane. Daphne got up and shut the open windows. "Lord, this damn rain. That mean no clothes will be washed tomorrow. Amy get off!" she sucked her teeth and came to the table.

"What you doing?" she asked Sandra, and sat down.

"I have to write something up."

"Mmh. You ever go to the cinema?"

"Yes, in Pheasant."

"We must go out together. I go to the cinema sometimes. I don't like to go too often though. Too many damn rowdies does sit in box and balcony now. Long ago this city used to be called the most beautiful in the West Indies. Look at it now. Ever since the British gone, nobody don't paint the buildings or look after them. And the city was more peaceful. You could go for a drive or a walk and move freely. Now, these damn pickpockets and limers take over the streets and cinemas. You must be careful when you riding out so late at night."

Sandra sat silent. Daphne was inviting conversation. Finally she asked her, "Might you leave the country, go abroad to live?"

Daphne gave her a puzzled look. "Me? I am Guianese. I can't live anywhere else."

Sandra regarded this as a bizarre statement. "But you just said you don't like the country anymore."

Daphne scowled at her; she did not care to have her contradictions, her confusions of values and identity mirrored back to her. It made her extremely angry when this happened.

Daphne frightened her a great deal; she was family, she was a woman alone; would she too grow so defensive and confused? The decay of her circumstances were so evident yet Daphne lived with a sense of superiority over the poor. She spoke as if with regret for the vanished past of colonial Georgetown, but also seemed desperate to escape from that past. Now she was trying to adapt to a different future, trying to believe it was one

103

which would include her. People like Daphne were hoping that somehow the British would return through the present government, now that the socialist Jagan government had been overthrown. She spoke of moral values but turned a blind eye to the connivance and corruption which the change of Government had involved.

Daphne rose and went to her bedroom, and shut the door.

The rain was pelting down now. She shut her eyes and listened to the pounding on the corrugated zinc roof. The cottage was cooling quickly, giving up its warmth. The entire city was being washed. Every noise was silenced, people subdued, when the rain stormed down like this. The roar of a car as it passed outside was heard as a gasp or sigh of a noise, muffled by the downpour.

She wrote up the report, a bare shell of description, aware that she was omitting the vulgar jokes, the insults and intimidations which had passed between the magistrate, superintendents and lawyers, and how, with these tactics, they had subdued and frightened the witnesses, especially the dead man's relatives, into dumb incomprehension. She wrote the last sentence: "The magistrate returned a verdict of misadventure." That sentence, the substance of her report, and the omissions about the intimidations, sat on her mind. They were three separate facts refusing to be joined together. In her report, she had copied the form of the court reports, each paragraph a series of factual statements about the participants, with a sprinkling of details about the content of the cross-examinations.

In the morning, the streets were wet and slippery. Pedestrians and cyclists were exposed to the splashes a car made as it cut through the sinks in hollow sections of the road. The clouds, tinged by grey, concealed the sun, and the air glowed with freshness. The heat and dust which had settled on the city during the last few days were washed away. The paint on the wooden buildings looked clean; the unpainted ones bare and sweated. Motorcycles banked dangerously at the roundabout near the cenotaph, their wheels spinning with water as they went, and drivers honked their car horns in irritation when the more lithe machines threaded through too close for comfort.

She was late getting in at the Mail. Stamp was standing near the editor's door when she came through the entrance.

"Miss Yansen, you did the Inquiry report?" he asked.

"It's hand-written," she said, drawing it from her handbag.

He took it. "I'll see you later about it," he said.

Bradley was fuming in the reporters' section. "Stamp now become unofficial Chief Reporter," he complained.

"Paul and Lewis in yet?" she asked.

He replied, "The editor got the two of them in there with him, dressing them down for something."

Paul and Lewis left the editor's office, deep in talk, their hands thrust into their trousers' pockets.

"What he tell you all?" Bradley demanded to know.

Stamp strode briskly from the editor's office, overtaking Paul and Lewis. He was holding her report. He put the report on her desk. "Miss Yansen, you have to cut this down to four hundred words. It too long. Your sentences too long too, and it's not factual enough. Also, we don't want the names of the policemen and witnesses not actually involved. Do the corrections and have it in by eleven."

"Stamp, come here," Bradley ordered.

Stamp hesitated. "I have work to do."

Bradley sucked his teeth in annoyance. "Man look, come here."

Stamp sauntered up to his desk. "What happen?"

Bradley held his hand and drew him closer. Their appearance was so similar they looked like brothers. He spoke with genuine affection, conspiratorially. "You turn the editor's hack?"

Stamp drew his hand away. "What you talking about?"

"You know very well what I talking about. We join the Mail together. We took great pride in thinking we would be writing for

105

ourselves. Now I see you writing for the editor, all kinda propaganda..."

Stamp sucked his teeth. "Don' talk nonsense. What you think you are, novelist? Nobody don' write fo' themselves on a newspaper. You write to a formula. Bradley, you trying to make mischief and cause confusion in this place. What happen? You jealous because the editor don't favour you?" Stamp turned and walked away.

Bradley pointed to Stamp as he went. "That fucking traitor," he commented.

"Leave Owen alone," Lewis muttered, sitting at his desk.

Bradley held up that day's Mail. "You see all his write-up today? Look, photograph and full name, everything, and lead story about the government's farming exploits in the interior. All lies."

"Somebody has to do it," Lewis said.

"What happen to you two in the editor's office?" Bradley asked.

Paul shrugged nonchalantly. "He didn't like this and that about our writing. Says we're not living up to our responsibility to the nation..."

"Not positive," Lewis added. "Too individualistic."

"What the shit all that mean?" Bradley fretted.

"Could mean anything," Lewis said.

"Oh no," Paul disagreed. "It mean only one thing. He want to control everything that goes into print. That man stinks. He trying to make us mentally uniform."

Lewis sighed. "Nobody can do that."

Paul wagged his finger at Lewis. "That is complacency, Mark."

Lewis sighed. "You try. You want to be hero. I taking it easy. I not getting involved."

"Lewis know which side his bread buttered on," Bradley commented spiritlessly.

Bradley was not really angry with Stamp for his lack of political morals, for politics did not really matter among them. It was a curious, violent male jealousy which Bradley possessed towards his male friends. Stamp belonged to him, he wanted him back in his male roost. He was angry that Stamp had flown to the editor. Bradley also overseered the mens' relationships with women. If he felt it was at all possible to destroy an attraction towards a woman he did it with a subtle savagery, by demolishing the woman's sexuality. He once commented that a woman to whom Stamp was attracted was 'nice and thick' and this was enough to reduce the woman's value. Stamp had attempted to live with someone once, a girl from a sheltered, religious family. Stamp could not induce her to sleep with him except by setting up a flat with her. After their first night together, Stamp complained bitterly, publicly about her shyness in bed but he did not think of it as sexual inexperience or shyness to which he ought to respond with tenderness. He reacted to it violently - it was a sin against his maleness, she had refused to be flattered by his prowess. Bradley shared Stamp's outrage and contempt for the girl; Lewis and Morgan did not. But they did not defend her. People like Morgan and Lewis did not like to admit to their sexual tyranny over women, they kept it secret, but when their male pride was ignored they could be as chauvinist as the rest. It was often very confusing because, having gone to Queen's College and St. Stanislaus, they knew how to feign responsibility when they wanted to. And they were also young and genuinely naive about themselves.

They worked despondently, calmly. She cut down her report. The more she did, the more her omissions lay like a sickness on her conscience. The editor had deleted the dead man's name, an Indian name, and replaced it with 'the deceased'. He had also deleted the names of the dead man's relatives. She remembered the barefooted group: country people, with their heads covered in worn hats and handkerchiefs, dressed in their best clothes, thick unironed khakis and cheap floral dresses all sewn in the same style. Their cowed, alienated faces crowded her memory. They had sat at the back of the room, looking like herded cattle, prodded into submission by the manipulations of the magistrate, superintendent and lawyers.

They, as young reporters fresh out of high school, had scribbled for their lives, for their bread and butter.

She read her original notes. They echoed the questions the magistrate had raised: a policeman shot a man; what was the truth behind this? Was it murder or an accident? Whichever, the circumstances around this situation had to be clarified. Who was the murdered man, who the policeman? Names, dates of birth and other background details about their lives were confirmed and reconfirmed by witnesses. Why were they at the sugar estate on the day of the shooting? Why were the workers demonstrating? Who were the sugar workers? How come there were whole families there? The magistrate had commented, "They musta been looking fo' bacchanal." Which police station did the policeman come from? How far was the police station from the scene of the demonstration? Who gave the orders for the policemen to go to the demonstration? Which officer issued firearms to the policemen? Was this officer acting on his own authority? Who gave orders about supervising the demonstration? How many people claimed they heard the superintendent give the order to open fire? Did the demonstrators attack the policemen? When last were the guns serviced? How old were these guns? How long was this corporal in the force? Was he a violent man? Who heard the shot? Who saw the deceased fall?

The magistrate had concluded that the gun had gone off accidentally when the corporal was jostled by a demonstrator. The deceased had met his death accidentally, and no compensation would be going to his relatives.

The Inquiry was prejudiced. The magistrate had hardly waited for an answer before he rattled off the next question, not bothering to meet the witnesses' eyes, except when he barked out a reproach. Paul said it happened all the time, that justice was a mockery, the lawyers courtroom decoration and that the public did not want to know the truth, only a few facts which would engage their interest briefly, and reassure them the trappings of justice seemed to exist.

She tore up her report, and spent the morning writing one which she knew the editor would not print. She criticized the magistrate's and lawyer's intimidatory behaviour, pointed out that questions were left unanswered and asserted that justice had not been done.

When she finished, she took it to the editor's office and left it with Mrs. Singh. The lunch break passed and the afternoon wore on, without a summons or approach from the editor. He made several appearances outside his office, and each time he did, she searched for some sign that he had read the article and had a reaction to it. But he seemed as impenetrable as ever.

It was almost four when Mrs. Singh came to the section and summoned everyone to the editor's office.

Stamp was installed at a small desk next to the editor's. He smoked casually, and kept his head down as he scribbled away.

"Hello Owen," Bradley greeted him.

He ignored Bradley. The editor did not look up when they filed in. A small fan, perched at an angle on the wall, ventilated the airless room. The windows were wire-meshed and shut. They waited awhile until the editor finished reading. When he raised his head, he drew a deep breath, sighed, and drew himself up in his chair. He took her report from the filing basket on his right and handed it to Paul.

"Mr. Morgan, do you know anything about this?" he asked.

Paul flicked the pages, looked at her, and read the report. "I don't understand the question, Sir. How could I know anything about this?"

The editor smiled behind his sunglasses. "Well, you know how we reporters function." His smile faded. "Show it to Mr. Bradley and Mr. Lewis."

Lewis and Bradley read the report, their faces impassive. The editor studied them closely, searching for their reactions.

When Bradley finished reading, the editor turned to her. "Miss Yansen, tell the truth. Did you really write that?"

Astounded, she repeated his question. "Did I write it?"

"Yes, you," the editor asserted.

Paul raised his hand. "Just a minute. What's going on? What are you getting at Mr. Editor. Of course Miss Yansen wrote the report. If she said she wrote it, she wrote it. I don't see any problems."

Stamp had stopped writing and was looking on at the scene. The editor sighed, sat back and spread his arms along the arms of his chair. He shook his head. "I am not a fool, Mr. Morgan."

Paul shifted in his chair. "I didn't say so."

The editor grunted and looked at Paul. "Tell me, Mr. Morgan, are you still having relations with Mr. Persaud?"

Paul frowned. "Me? Why I should still be having relations with Mr. Persaud? I don't understand the question."

The editor turned and flicked a switch on the wall. The fluorescent bulb on the ceiling flickered then lit. The room was washed with its transparent light. It held them in stark, blunt images. Their skins, each a different hue, looked equally exposed, flat, textureless.

Bradley shuffled restlessly. "What's the point of these strange questions?" he demanded, impatient.

The editor turned to him, "I am a man like you, Mr. Bradley. I want answers to questions. I have as little time to waste as you." He looked at his watch. "I have a family to go home to. I am only here to do an honest day's job. Let me get to the point." Lewis was still holding the report. He stretched out his hand for it. He tore it to shreds and dropped it into the wastepaper basket. Then he turned to her. "Miss Yansen, so much for your report, if it was your work."

Paul cut in, "I don' understand why you keep implying it isn't Miss Yansen's work."

The editor ignored him. "As I said, I have no time to waste. Don't play games with me, Mr. Morgan. Certain troublesome elements have been removed from this office, but I see little embers are still alive in their wake. Let me tell you all, I will not tolerate subversion and treason..."

Bradley burst out laughing. "I see what is happening..."

"I will thank you not to interrupt me when I am saying something important, Mr. Bradley. Now I believe someone put

110

up someone to write that report, and brought it in here purporting that it was written by Miss Yansen..."

She insisted, "I wrote it, I wrote the report myself. I don't understand how you come to such a conclusion..."

He silenced her. "That is quite enough from you, Miss Yansen. I will thank you not to speak. I don't want to hear another word from you."

"But I wrote it!" she declared, her voice rising.

The editor slapped the desk. "Dammit, when I speak, don't contradict me! You hear?" He got up and kicked his chair away. "Now go home, all of you! Let me remind you that you are not in the least bit indispensable. Goddamit! You don't know when you're lucky to have a damn job! I tell you, I will have no qualms about firing the entire pack of you. Now leave!"

The men exchanged looks of incredulity, then silently turned and left the office. She hung back, opened her mouth to speak, but the editor shouted, "Go!"

Outside the editor's door, Bradley howled with mirth. The building was empty and echoed with his noise. They made their way outside to their bicycles.

"Miss Yansen," Bradley said, "you stir up a marabunta nest." His face was bright with mirth. "You know I never see the editor in such a state." His look became serious. "You all think he mad or something? The man sound like he was going to have a nervous breakdown. Now, tell me, why Persaud ever wanted to take such a man seriously. People like that are not worth fighting at all. You not fighting against ideas there, only paranoia."

They were relieved. They wore relaxed smiles as they unlocked their cycles, and pushed them along the path, an extra spring in their step.

"Sandra, we should give you a medal for that," Lewis commented.

"I don't want a medal. I didn't want to be involved with the lying."

Bradley patted her shoulder. "Don't be so damn serious. I think you do it for a joke. Look man, let's go to the Tropicana for a drink and celebrate. After what happen with Persaud, that place was beginning to nauseate me. But I think I can work there now. After all, the editor only a paranoid jackass. That is all power is, paranoia."

"Don't talk so big, Bradley. The editor not the man power with. He is only a puppet, a little one. Just because the joke on him once, you must not underestimate him..."

"Awright, Paul, awright. We know you're clever."

The cottage was locked up. A letter from Jay lay on the mat. She opened the windows and sat down to read; Helen was all right; there would be no operation; it had been a false alarm; there was no need to come home.

The silence and emptiness in the cottage was depressing after the drama and conflict in the office. Tomorrow, things would return to normal there. More conflicts and insults lay ahead with the editor. Bradley had been happy that afternoon because he had seen how easily the situation in the office could turn absurd, how it could be spiced with anarchy, the editor undermined. To Bradley, that was a game that could be played forever. It was the brightest future he could look forward to. Paul was more worried by the serious implications of the situation. Persaud's imprisonment hung like a stone around his neck. He equated incarceration with murder, the denial of freedom with death, as if one would lead naturally to the other. Paul was unmoved by the editor's vulnerability. He refused to view him in any way which would lead him to feel the slightest pang of sympathy or humour.

The telephone rang. It was David. He wanted to take her to a party. She accepted the invitation.

He called on time, looking immaculate again. They drove towards Bel Air Park. He was in good spirits, looking forward to the party. He said he was glad she could come; now, she would meet all his colleagues and friends, 'real people' he called them. David was a man convinced he was living in the future, with others like himself.

The house was luxurious, a two-storeyed bungalow with a

spacious lawn all around. A tall hibiscus hedge provided privacy from the narrow street; mango and dwarf coconut trees bordered the lawn round the back and sides. The properties here were closely adjoined.

The guests sat or stood around the open, sheltered verandah behind the house. The coloured lights, strung along the rafters and the rails of the verandah, softened the setting. Light music drifted indoors; a breeze ruffled the trees. Compared to Daphne's cottage, this was a larger, more open island of comfort. The grass grew tall and uncut and untended in Daphne's yard; here men and women sat on wrought-iron white chairs on the close-cut lawn, or walked along tinkling the ice in their glasses as they talked.

He took her to the bar. A middle-aged, tired-looking man in an ill-fitting white jacket, white shirt, black bow tie and black trousers with red edging running down the sides served their drinks.

"Evening, Mr. Petrie," he greeted David.

"Hello, Tak," David returned. "Get me a double whisky and the lady a rum punch."

"Coming right up, Sir."

"David!" a woman's voice shrieked, and a small thin woman in a tight black dress, her small breasts half-exposed by the low neckline, came to him and, pressing herself against him, kissed his cheeks, scrutinized her and said, "Who is this, your latest girl?"

Unabashed, David beamed and introduced them. Her name was Maureen Wilkins, and she was the daughter of the Vice-President of the Junior Chamber of Commerce. She also worked with Fitzpatrick's, the auditors.

"Where you work?" Maureen Wilkins demanded.

"At the Daily Mail," she replied.

"You know Mrs. Hart, the manager's wife?"

She had seen Mr. Hart walking about in the office, but never laid eyes on his wife. Their conversation ended there.

David led her to a small group on the edge of the lawn, near the verandah. He introduced her to two of his colleagues,

113

middle-aged men; their wives; a lawyer; a B.W.I.A. pilot and his fiancee; a doctor and his wife, who taught at St. Rose's High School. The B.W.I.A. pilot was dominating the conversation. They were debating the merits of flying B.O.A.C. as opposed to flying B.W.I.A. It was a heated debate, with no one getting the upper hand, but many tales of agonies suffered through B.W.I.A. incompetence weighing against the pilot.

"You ever travelled B.O.A.C., girl?" the pilot's fiancee enquired, and when she replied that she hadn't, the death toll of their conversation sounded again, as it had with Maureen Wilkins.

She sat silent among them for an hour, until David, throwing worried glances in her direction, leaned close and whispered, "Don' look so serious, make small talk."

The conversation turned from flying to banking facilities, holidays abroad, cars, clothes and their children.

The music was turned up indoors, the lights turned off and couples formed around the floor, swaying to the music.

"Is time for us old fogeys to go home," one of David's middle-aged colleagues declared, rising and stretching. "Time for the young people to take over." But he did a jig to the music and peals of laughter shook the group.

As they made their way indoors, the editor emerged from the darkness, along the path leading from the front gate, round the house to the lawn. He wore his dark glasses, a fresh white shirt and brown trousers; a cigarette smoked from his lips.

"There's your boss, Peters," David commented.

"I didn't know you knew him," she said.

"Everybody know Peters," David returned. "He like pot salt, in everything. I don' know him to talk to. He's not that sort of fellow. You just know him, that's all."

She kept her eyes on the editor while they joined the bulky shadows of the couples who were now dancing. The editor went to the bar, got himself a drink, and stood alone, looking all around him.

"I don't get the feeling you enjoying yourself," David commented, holding her close.

The dancers were the younger people. The older guests had drifted away. A few lingered outside on the lawn, and it was towards these the editor eventually gravitated. He went from one couple to another, exchanged brief words, then, as quickly as he had appeared, he disappeared.

David did not see at all the drama of the editor's presence at this party. He, like many of the young people there, the professional people, the airline and embassy staff, did not yet see the need, as someone like Daphne had done, to court the likes of the editor. David was too young and arrogant to see that people like him would need to learn to live with a future being fabricated by the editors of this world.

When the couples ceased dancing, they sat in a circle on chairs placed against the walls round the room, tinkling the ice in their glasses, their voices and laughter lacing the music. A comfortable lethargy set in, helped by the drink and the dragging music. Over David's shoulder she could see a couple locked in a tight embrace, another writhing in a darkened corner. Eventually the coloured lights on the verandah were switched off, and the love-making among the couples intensified.

Her resistance to his tightening embraces irritated him. When she sat out on the dancing, he sprawled on a chair near her, frigid with disappointment.

In an instant, the music switched from American and British pop music to calypsoes which sprayed the darkened room and the dancers broke and leapt about, flinging their arms wide, gyrating their bodies and chanting the familiar choruses. When she refused to dance, he sought out Maureen Wilkins, and she spent the next hour watching their antics.

It was getting on to two a.m. when the lights came on and exposed couples sprawled around the room, sweaty and crumpled, flushed with drink and weakened with exhaustion. The irrepressible fanned their flagging spirits with obscene jokes, throwing these across the room like a bouncing ball, until their voices were hoarse from laughing and competing.

They wore out the limits of their wit and teetered on the edge of boredom. Just when the party seemed about to break up, with some hinting it was time to go home, a nude apparition appeared on the inner stairs which led to the upper storey: he was David's age, in his early twenties, sparse hair decorating his thin chest, thicker along his lower arms and legs; his trunk and thighs a uniform brown hue, his face, arms and neck darker. He grinned drunkenly, his eyes hooded and red. He wore only a sanitary belt around his waist, and a sanitary napkin which barely concealed his genitals.

The group, taken aback at first, began to hoot and whistle derisively. The men roused themselves first, leaped on him and dragged him down the stairs. They slapped his buttocks and snapped the elastic, threatening to take belt and pad off. Dazed, he allowed himself to be passed around, teased and admired. Then the women joined in, hugging and kissing him as if he were a baby.

David was doubled up with helpless laughter near her, tears streaming from his eyes. She rose, left the room and went to sit alone on the lawn.

Outdoors it was a beautiful night, the deep purple sky fretted with stars, the city washed by moonlight. She thought of Ben and Helen and the house in Pheasant. It would be quiet with life there. She missed them. It was not homesickness that she felt, but longing for their greater simplicity. Frustration polluted and wasted them too, but not to the point of the wilful dissipation she was witnessing.

David swayed drunkenly from the house. He came to her, and held her shoulders in a warm grip. "You want to go home?" he slurred.

"Yes, I want to go home," she said. "But can you drive?"

"Course I can drive," he yelled. "I can do anything, anything!"

He drove dumbly and uncertainly, managing to keep the car on a straight course. Daphne's tiny cottage looked welcoming in the moonlight. He was so drunk and exhausted, he was lost to the world, all dissipated flesh, as she must appear too, she thought, in his eyes. He peered at her and mumbled "Good

116

Night," falling forward to hang on to the door and drag it shut, as if he were bringing down a final wall between them, his eyeballs turned inwards not seeing her.

David did not call again.

One week replaced another, lengthened into months and the dramas in the office, streets and Daphne's cottage smoothed into routines.

Rising in the mornings, cycling through the streets, meeting the reporters each day, it was as if the newspaper, which she had read in Pheasant, had itself come to life. Small and large events were trapped in type, compressed and reduced to print on paper. It happened in the factory-like office. Beyond its four walls lay the outside world: parliament, courts, business places, the civil service and the schools. The reporters grew expert at packaging it all, honed to routine, dulled to the editor's manipulations once they had seen through them.

Bradley's rages and obscenities often exploded in the office and shattered its lethargy like a hand thrust through a sheet of newspaper, sudden and violent. Lewis was his opposite. He pored over his work. All his energies were concentrated on it. And his politeness came, like Bradley's rages, from another world of feeling. As remote too was Paul's despairing banter, which replaced his earlier gloom. Each was detached, in his own way, from the world they reported on.

The editor confined them to the office, he and Stamp sharing the outside assignments, helped in their task by what they called their 'reliable sources'.

Persaud was released from jail, and now lived in exile in Barbados. Without his leadership there was no opposition, and the freedom which they had felt the editor threatened ceased to be a real issue. Without him everyone waited for a new future to unfold itself.

When they worked late in the office, their talk and laughter echoed round the building. They often cycled home in pairs, when the day was cooled, the shops shut. Beyond the wharves, beyond Kingston, the Atlantic Ocean surged powerfully. It could be heard only at that time of the day, around the rim of the city, with the traffic gone, the crowds absent and only the beggars and the Tiger Bay residents about. The smells of the ocean and the warehouses on the wharf hung in the air, the salty musky air of dusty streets, sea, airless shops, ships' holds and greasy steamers. The blast of a ship's horns as it made its way in and out of the harbour found no echo along the streets. The crowded coastline sent it back across the water, like the seagull's cries, to be swallowed up by the sky.

Behind the shore, the city centre was a magnet, drawing movement to itself. It was like entering Georgetown from the East Coast, when the country air dropped behind, and the close heat of the centre of Georgetown closed in: the life of business, the civil service, courtrooms, Stabroek and Bourda markets, and the slums which stretched from La Penitence through Albouystown to Tiger Bay; marooned inhabitants wedged into rotting cottages and narrow streets.

Leaving Water Street, they would cycle into the wide-angled, tilting roundabout where the streets split off from the junction, past the facades of houses, shops and cinemas ranged in close, uneven lines.

Drawn deeper into the maze of streets, the domesticity of the city showed in a curtain lifting in the breeze at an open window, children playing in the yards, people sitting out on the verandahs. The cinemas, cake shops, grocery stores provided focus to the swirl of movement. The beggar, the drunk, the gangsters, the youthful and the more mature, were as permanent a fixture as those who sought pleasure in the old colonial hotels with all-night bars and weekend dance-bands.

Letters from home and reports from the country areas spoke of more unrest on the sugar estates. There were prolonged strikes, struggles between the rival unions, management and workers. The old revolutionary union had been driven back to its base on

118

the estates, the final blows to its influence in Georgetown being delivered by a union which had received funding from unions in the United States. There was talk too that the Daily Mail had received funds from the C.I.A. Only on the sugar plantations was the old struggle still going on. The people there were still fighting British domination while Georgetown was renewing its relationship with the British, and entering into a new one with the government of the United States, both anxious to prevent Guiana becoming another Cuba. And in Pheasant the struggle between the union which had supported the old government and this new combination of enemies shook the foundations at home. Ben wrote to say that things had never been so bad: he had to close the shop some afternoons for lack of stock. Food and money were scarce in the villages.

Lewis became engaged and talked of leaving for Canada where most of his family now lived. Paul and Bradley were trying to get visas to the United States. Sandra turned her mind to thoughts about the university, and wrote home to ask Ben and Helen what they thought about her going there. They wrote back to say that if she thought it the best course to take, she should take it.

Paul's visa came through and a farewell party was arranged for him at Stamp's house.

Stamp, his mother, his two sisters, Lewis and his girlfriend were the only people there when she arrived. The women sat in a row on a settee. Stamp introduced her to them. His younger sister, Lily, was still at high school; his older sister, Veronica, was preparing to go to the University of the West Indies in Jamaica. Lewis introduced her to his girlfriend, Mary, who was a secretary with Bookers.

"I know you," Mary said, "I saw you at Bookers' store once with David Petrie."

Sandra glanced at Lewis, but he avoided her eyes.

"Oh," Mrs. Stamp joined in, "So you're David Petrie's girlfriend. I know his family in Trinidad you know, from hearing

119

about them. His father is a lawyer, and I think his mother have some French in her. David is a very nice boy."

"I hardly know him," Sandra protested.

"I hear he's going back to Trinidad soon though," Stamp's older sister said.

Sandra said nothing, and the conversation between them turned to Veronica's impending departure for Jamaica. They turned over the details of the arrangements for her departure, like fussy wives picking a chicken bone dry. Mrs. Stamp was a big woman with large arms. Her wiry hair was pulled upwards in a bun. Her eyes were grey, her nose thin and pointed. She sat squarely, her large form heavy on the cushion. She listened keenly to the girls, laughing when they laughed, and sometimes injecting a mild comment or question. Carol, Stamp's girlfriend, was not as excitable as Stamp's sisters, who were constantly disagreeing and tripping over their words in their haste to out-talk each other. Carol and Veronica had gone to high school together. Carol stabilised their talk with a sensible fact or occasional comment and her sensible questions. In this house too it was the future that was being picked over like a juicy bone.

Paul and Bradley arrived with a large party of young couples, some of the printing press operators, the messenger boys and one of the delivery van drivers among them. The room was suddenly full and lively with talk. Paul apologised for being late and shook Mrs. Stamp's hand. Bradley stood in the corner of the small sitting room, arms folded and watched Stamp's family with his familiar stare. Someone started the record player. A few couples began dancing. Bradley told people to sit on the floor as there weren't enough chairs. The men passed a bottle of rum around. In the half-dark room, Sandra saw Mrs. Stamp, her two daughters and Carol get up and go to a bedroom. She sat on the settee opposite Lewis. Bradley, Paul and Stamp joined them. The music was turned up louder; Bradley asked her to dance.

As they danced, her eyes searched in the dark room to recognise individuals amongst the shadows, but only the music

120

was there, sweeping the room. Bradley, never carried away by the music, economized on his movements, head held high, limbs co-ordinated, his spectacles flashing back the dim coloured points of the lights in the room. He held her lightly during the slow music, his palm firm on her back, and when they danced apart, he one-stepped efficiently. Paul danced with closed eyes of ecstasy whatever the music. The dancing stopped while paper plates of chow mein and bottles of soft drinks were passed around. Then Otis Redding's 'Sitting on the Dock of the Bay,' drew the couples together again.

In the wake of the party, departing voices echoed down the street. The room seemed amazed by the sudden quiet. The floorboards were ravaged by scratches. The smell of beer lingered. Sandra, Stamp, Paul and Bradley were sitting on the verandah when three latecomers arrived.

"Sorry we're late man," one of the three apologised. "We had to go to another party, and didn't figure you folks would round off so early."

Paul introduced Maurice Dodd, Winston Harris and Son Young. Maurice Dodd was on holiday from U.W.I.; Winston Harris had just graduated and Son Young was a primary school teacher. Stamp and Paul fetched them food, drinks and chairs.

Now Veronica returned from the bedroom and began to fuss over the older men. "Maurice, would you like another plate of chow mein?"

Dodd was flattered. He rubbed his stomach slowly. "Girl, I would love another plate of your chow mein..."

Harris laughed. "With plenty pepper sauce, girl."

"You all miss the Guianese pepper sauce bad in Jamaica, eh?" This was Mary, Lewis's girlfriend who was shyer, a little overawed by the two university men.

Harris responded, "Pepper sauce and you Guianese girls."

Harris and Dodd laughed together and so did Veronica.

121

They were flirting because Veronica was soon going to become one of them, soon to go to university in Jamaica too. But it excluded the others who had nothing else to look forward to.

Mary went to sit with Lewis in his shell-shaped chair. He made room for her and she nestled up to him with difficulty. They were a picture of closeness.

Paul asked Dodd, "So what you like best about Jamaica, Maurice?"

Harris and Dodd exchanged mischievous schoolboy grins and Dodd asked Harris playfully, "You think we should tell them, Winston? You think we should give away our secret?"

Harris chuckled deeply. "I don' know if we should corrupt nice Guianese people, boy Maurice. They shouldn't be exposed to our bad Jamaican ways we pick up."

But Dodd was going to tell them anyway. He declared, "The three W's I like best about Jamaica."

Stamp was the only one to sense a good laugh in the offing. He encouraged Dodd. "The three W's?"

Harris exploded into laughter. He was Dodd's Fool. Dodd told the jokes, Dodd played macho, Dodd took the initiative and claimed all the attention and Harris was there in the background to give Dodd's ego encouragement and support it in all sorts of ways, by giggling, laughing, sneering or doubling up with mirth while Dodd timed his own jokes, took his time bringing them to a climax. They were a team, an inseparable pair.

Veronica was back on the verandah again with two plates of chow mein and a bottle of pepper sauce. As she poured pepper sauce she resumed her flirtation with them. Every response to Veronica was shared by the two men, they reacted to her as one. Veronica did not bother to offer anyone else chow mein.

Bradley was lying in the hammock strung up in one corner of the verandah. He was observing the flirtation between Dodd, Harris and Veronica cooly. He asked in a matter-of-fact voice, which Sandra knew well enough only feigned interest and flattery, "What's this three W's?" This was the voice Bradley used when he was laying a trap for a victim. He did it all the time at the Daily Mail.

122

The university men took his interest to be genuine. Harris, his mouth full, nudged Dodd. "Tell them, Maurice. The suspense is too much."

Dodd shook his head sagely. "No man."

Harris insisted. "Yes man. Is your duty as an educated son of Guiana."

Bradley drawled, "But of course."

Dodd now assented. He placed his empty plate on the floor, swallowed a mouthful of beer, wiped his lips with a handkerchief and said, "All right."

The orchestration of the joke was ending. Resolution was imminent. "You all ready?" Harris asked.

Stamp said, "Yes man."

Together, Harris and Dodd chanted triumphantly, "Wine, Women and Weed!" Then they almost fell off their chairs laughing.

Stamp laughed too but Son Young got up and left the verandah. Paul kept a serious face and so did Mary and Lewis. Mary and Lewis drew even closer together. Bradley sneered, not openly, and a little smugly because he had caught the university men in his trap and they did not see it. If Harris and Dodd noticed any muted disapproval, they would attribute it to the prudery of their home town from which they had escaped and it would be another cause for them to feel superior. Veronica was discomfited. Within a matter of minutes she had been flirted with, treated as an equal who could be admitted to their company, their group, even share their status. Now she was an outcast, only a woman who, like wine and ganga, was to be consumed for the pleasure of men. But she was stubborn. She sighed, "Lord, you all too wicked." Then quickly left the verandah.

Bradley smirked at Veronica's departing figure and returned his attention to Dodd and Harris as two of the three electric bulbs on the verandah went out. "So how you boys finding the home town?" Bradley asked.

"I mean to ask you all that," Harris said. "I been away so long. I been asking people about the race riots, man. First thing I leave home to go to U.W.I., and hear these strange things on the radio. Race riots at home! And although it so long ago now, I still not happy with this business. Is like if a father or mother die while you're away, and you can't come home for the funeral, and when you do come home, that same, empty, helpless, puzzling feeling all over the place. Like missing an important, personal piece of history. So here I home four years later, and I watch this place and say: Well yes, no, I can't believe this thing happen. I refuse to believe it happen. Man look, I was upset bad. People in Jamaica were upset, and I understand people here were very distressed by the whole thing. The day I got the news in Jamaica, I stayed glued by the radio whole day, panicking. What the hell went on man?"

"People were afraid," Lewis said, "panicking. I stayed in my room. But I could hear the sirens and people running in the street, and shouting. It was strange - just noises, sometimes a group or groups of people passing on the street, sometimes just muttering, sometimes a fire engine tearing down the road, and the British army jeeps and trucks roaring past. And all day, the thick smoke from the buildings burning in Water Street like a fat cloud touching from earth to sky. Now and then you'd hear somebody telling somebody else in the street that somebody got beaten up, or that people were fighting in some street." Mary drew away from him a little as he spoke.

Harris shook his head in disbelief. The moonlight washed the sky with a blue tinted light, and slanted onto the verandah. The moon was behind the tall tree in the yard, and the shadow of the tree fell onto the verandah too: a curious skeletal shape. Their faces and bodies were pasted with the light and shadows. The breeze rustling the tree, their slight, shifting movements mobilised the fall of the patterns, so for a moment someone was visible in the clear, strange light, then splayed distorted by the shadow of a leafy branch.

"I was in Berbice," Sandra said. "It was far away, but very close. The mood affected the people. I was listening to the radio too. People stayed home. People came to our shop and argued with each other. They were confused. They didn't seem to

124

understand what exactly was going on in Georgetown. I wasn't sure what was fact and what was rumour. It was all frustration with not knowing what was going on. I never seen some people get so excited or angry. There was talk of murders on the East Coast, and rumours that bands of people were crossing the river to come and stir up trouble in Canefields. Some even said the fire would spread across the river and come to Berbice."

"It was all politics, man," Paul said. "Those damn politicians as usual. Scamps. They stir up and ferment the people, but no-one blames them for it publicly. They just say Guiana has race problems. Is politician problem we have. Then when all the destruction and violence finish, those scamps come out from hiding and make long pious speeches. You're right girl. This feeling of not being sure exactly what was going on was strong. It change life since. All the little patterns of living during the long strike stay - even the times the postman deliver letters, and it strengthen racial feelings, sanction it with history and make sure it will always be around. Look, even some academics at the University here and at U.W.I. frame what they say in racial terms nowadays. Race is God's word, not the doing of a pack of scamps anymore. The newspaper and the politician speeches are what the people go by, because they afraid to think for themselves. Now and then, you'll hear some sense in a cake shop, or at a street corner, in some private conversation. But public life is very surreal."

"I would agree with you about the politicians," Harris said, "but I can't picture the Guianese people doing the things they did. It all so unreal to me."

"Well, it was real here," Bradley said. "What things you can't picture the Guianese people doing?"

"How you mean?" Harris asked. "Looting. Burning. Beating. Raping. I hear young children get beaten. And Wismar - I hear the most terrible stories about what went on there. Those things not in Guianese people nature."

"Guianese people?" Bradley asked. "Who's Guianese people? I'm Guianese people. You're Guianese people. Paul is Guianese people. Lewis is Guianese people, and all the rest of us sitting here and drinking beers and discussing the race riot. You want to know what was happening? I been looting in Water Street, you been listening to your radio in Jamaica, Lewis was locked up in his room, Paul musta been locked up in his room writing poems, Stamp musta been screwing some whore in Water Street for twenty-five cents, and she musta been preferring to be looting in Water Street. All them poor people were beating up each other and looting left, right and centre. Men on East Coast chop up each other. Women get raped all over the place. The politicians call each other names. The civil servants show their true colours and behave like a herd of idiots. A lotta people were more worried about their property than who get killed, beaten or raped. Afterwards, everybody hold their heads and bawl to bring back the British Governor. Never mind the British army been pointing guns at the whole nation, on certain politicians' behalf, the same ones who talk about throwing off 'the shackles of colonialism' now. At the end of it, every man jack belly was full with looting, violence, hate, and the politicians too - British and Guianese - satisfied with the disaster they stir up. It was easy to lead the people after that, because they show what a pack of cowards and butchers they were, and how easy it was to manipulate them. What subject you studying? Drama? Sociology? Politics? History? English? All this is rich material for study you know. You can draw a lot out of it. After all, that's the story of our life. Plunder. We don' know how to put back anything, only how to take out. You can write you' thesis and get a Ph.D. for it. Make what sense it please you to make of it. Blame who you want to blame, excuse who you want to excuse. Give who you want a bad name. Find the safest answer most convenient to you. Find a scapegoat - that's the name of the game. The situation is rich - for comedy, intellectual speculation, drama, sociology. Take your pick."

Dodd and Harris exchanged meaningful looks, and shook their heads.

"This country needs leadership," Dodd said, "new leadership and young blood."

"Young blood like yours?" Bradley asked.

"Me? I'm only a teacher chappie," Dodd replied.

"What you teach?" Bradley asked.

"English," Dodd replied.

"I wouldn't mind teaching English," Bradley said. "I wouldn't mind studying and teaching it. I used to think I would write a novel."

Paul laughed. "Write a novel? Bradley, you know what you saying?" he asked. "If you write one, make sure it not too true. Dress it up nice. Season it with comedy, or else you in for a lot of mud-slinging. Boy, you asking for punishment, yes. Look at Bradley - he want to level down the society, plus write a novel. God, that's punishment, yes."

"Morgan," Bradley said, "your trouble is you gone cynical in your youth."

"You should study and teach English if that's what you want to do," Dodd told Bradley.

"No man," Bradley said. "I thought about it. It don't make no sense to me. What you do when you get B.A., or M.A. or Ph.D.? Is mainly a way of getting position, yes, in the end. Good for your self-respect and sense of achievement, yes. Part of every man for himself ethic. Looting was a useful experience. You know you looting, not fooling yourself. But looting is a way of life really, all the time, only some people have it sanctioned by the snobbery in the society. Look, we got our own university now. Where you going to put all these educated people to live side by side with the uneducated people? I know some of these fellows when they were shirt-tail in the nigger-yard. The first thing they doing when they get degree is buying big car, house, and getting wife and child. Setting up a comfortable, nouveau riche, bourgeois life style. No man, I couldn't be part of that. The poor people I come from still around. I would feel very schizophrenic in my big car, and seeing my friends and family hustling in the city, seeing my grandmother hobbling round on she big-foot at Bourda Market. I have family who lecture at the University you know. They like to talk about the good and the bad of people. Which people these people talking about I ask myself? University teach them to distance their own people from them, patronise their own people. No man, I love my people. I couldn't do that. I couldn't write and talk about my people as if I'm not one of them. You all in' no different than them missionaries and Christians that come down here preaching to camouflage the plunder going on all the time. You can't fool me because I greedy bad, like you. I want the same money they spending on you all so-called education. I want all them money they paying you all when you graduate, the money you spend on cars and petrol and big house - all that money that maintaining slavery. Doing good is you all hobby, but I in' your toy, and I resent it when you use poor people as your toys."

"You finish?" Dodd asked Bradley. "You finish? Let me ask you something. If you're one of the poor people you making speech for, what you doing lying down in somebody else's hammock, drinking somebody else's beer, and eating somebody else's food? Why you not out there now catching hell with them choke and rob boys and them prostitutes in Main Street? Why you not out there catching hell with them unemployed youths with the police breathing down their necks? I hear you're a reporter. Why you pushing pen on paper instead of a wheelbarrow in Stabroek Market? How many poor people could cock up their backsides in some hammock that don't belong to them and make speeches and eat and drink other people food? You should haul your ass out of that hammock and go and find a more worthwhile job, do some real work. You know what you really are? A big time parasite. Yes! I interested in education - very interested. I interested in the children yes - very interested. I thinking about the future you see. It don't serve me no cause and purpose to keep them ignorant. You really enjoy your speech. Everybody come in for it except you. You talk about thieves, murderers and whores as if they're people? Yes, they're people. More important they're destroyed souls, lost souls. Nothing romantic about that. You may think you're one of them. You don't know what it is to be a destroyed soul. You only want fuel for your fire, and you plunder poor people too for it. You damn right about plundering being a way of life. You don't even realise you doing it. I can't do anything much for these peo-

128

ple who gone down the drain, but I could think of doing something for the future to prevent it happening if it's possible. I not saying I'm right. I living on hope and faith. Things might not change in my lifetime, and even if they do, I can't be sure it's right, only better than things were before because it don't take such a toll on people's dignity. And I might never get near doing the smallest thing about it. But I'm not worried that I'm still a slave. That sound like your problem. You must be the greatest double-thinker of all time. You back-pedalling in the other direction, going your own way to prove you're not a slave. You pulling the wool over people's eyes, not we. You think you're unique? Look man, you bore me. At this point I lost interest with you. I finish with you."

"You might finish," Bradley said, "but not me. I won' finish till I six feet under. I see something dangerous in you. People disposable to you. A whole living mass of people you already dispose of in your mind as 'lost souls'. You done do all your paperwork about past, present and future. I hope the past and present don't catch up with you while you planning for the future. Is your lack of imagination that's dangerous."

"Bradley, change the subject now," Paul said.

"No," Lewis said. "Go on, Bradley. Let the man talk. I agree with him."

"You talk, Lewis!" Bradley retorted, angry. "You talk, damn you! Is your turn to talk. The man from the university just relegate me to the grave, never mind I alive and kicking. You talk with him. Let me hear you so when the time come I know what to do with you pious scamps. Your sort parasite off anything - including other people's thinking. You lose the ability to even think for yourself, you so damn secure. You talk and plan your perfect world. Come on, Morgan, talk. But you running away abroad tomorrow. Come on, you all talk. You all read the existentialists, talk about the art of preserving the self. You all lost your tongues? This situation very clear. Good night."

Back in her room in Daphne's cottage, her mind still swirling from the talk of the party, Sandra was dreaming. She saw the canefields as they were on a still, sunny Sunday when the children bathed and swam in the canal. The children were sitting in a group under the bridge which offered shade from the sun. Sometimes, one of them broke away from the group and dived into the water. The children were talking and laughing. The water tasted of ripe cane and the bed of the canal, laden with old cane, was springy to the touch of feet and hands. A fight broke out among the children.

"Ai!" a voice was calling from the bridge. The shadow falling from above onto the surface of the rippling canal was Lalta's, the watchman. "Al'y'u playing nakedskinness down deh? Al'y'u playing big man and woman?"

Everyone dived into the water and swam away, except her. Lalta leaned over the bridge and peered down at her.

"Eh, eh!" he exclaimed. "Ben daughta? You playin' big woman with y'u growing bubby at the door? You wait! I going tell y'u Daddy now, and see if he don't cut y'u tail! Don' le' me catch you playing he' again with all y'u bubby at the door, or else me' go cut am off..."

The dream fled as she heard a voice calling her name softly in the night at the back door. She looked at the clock near her bed. It was three a.m. She got out of bed and looked through the window. A man, she recognised him as Bradley, was sitting on the landing, doubled over.

"Bradley, what you want?" she asked.

"Open the door man," he said.

She switched on the landing light. He showed her his left arm. A deep, fresh gash ran from his shoulder to his elbow. The sleeve of his shirt was torn and soaked with blood. His face was wet with sweat, and he was without his spectacles. His eyes were wide with shock and fear.

"Them boys cut me," he said, "and I want some money bad."

"Which boys cut you?" she asked.

"Some boys in Main Street," he replied.

"Wait here," she said, "I'll bring some hot water and Dettol."

He took the bowl of cloudy water from her and cleaned his wound. His hand shook. He wound the bandage round his arm.

"I want some money bad," he said. "You have two hundred?"

"Two hundred?"

"Look," he said, "is either yes or no. I'll pay you back."

"Is all I have," she said. "For my university fees."

"I said I would pay you back," he said.

"When?"

"Jesus girl, I get a girl into trouble. Somebody will fix it up for two hundred. If I don' do it, she done for. I can' mind her. She can' mind no child."

"Who is the girl?"

"Tha's none of your business. Why you want to know?"

"Look, Bradley, you asking me for money to send a woman maybe to her grave, or to maim her. You asking me for money to take a life. I never had to think about such a thing. You bring it to me and expect me to hand you money for such a thing. Bradley, you think I am here only to make demands on. I have problems too. You think you have power over life and death? That money is for my life. Why I should use it to kill a life?"

"I don' want no long lecture. Please don't preach. O.K. I begging, is beg I begging. You want me to kiss y'u foot? Jesus, why you love to make me feel inferior? Women like you cut a man balls off..."

"Bradley, fo' God's sake shut up. You think you know me but you don't know me. You take me for one of those Georgetown girls who always snob you, but I not one of them. We can't seem to talk any sense. I don't think you see my point at all. I can stand up here and talk and talk, and I swear you will not hear me. You have a fixed idea about me. I have, and you don't have, and you want. O.K. Bradley. I am going to give you the money, but I will tell you why. Because you are so frightened, and because I am frightened that you are frightened. It's your life that comes first. All right. I will give you the money, but never ask me for anything else again and don't think I ever owed you anything or still owe you anything."

The next morning, Paul called in at the newspaper office on his way to the airport.

He shook everyone's hands and cracked jokes. She followed him to the waiting taxi outside.

"All alone you going to the airport," she commented.

"I was born alone," he said. "This isn't my choice I tell myself. But I fooling myself. All these years I live with Tina, my grandmother, and it was like we di'n' have no choice but to live with each other. My parents went to the States, and they were separated for a long time. Now, in their old age, they reunite and they say they ready to live with their son. How you like that? But I glad they reunite. And besides, I curious to see Big Bad America." He smiled. "Never mind I in' see Pheasant. Maybe one a' these days when I come back, if I come back. Time is queer, eh?"

He was very anxious. She said, "Don't be afraid, Paul. You're the first one of us to go. That takes courage."

He smiled and looked around. A woman was paying him a compliment and he was wondering what the others would think about it before he could accept it.

She changed the subject. "I wonder what we'll be like when we're old and grey. You think we'll mellow? You think Guiana will be alright?"

"You'll probably have dozens of grandchildren sitting round you when I see you again. Who's this mystery man I hear you talking on the phone with? You never told me." He had ignored the question about Guiana.

"That finished long ago."

"Never mind. Look after yourself. I don' know what else to tell you. I hope you like the university. Do your best."

"You saw Bradley?" she asked.

"Yes, this morning. I see he got cut bad. He'll be all right.

132

He's licking his wound. Got the fright of his life. Don' take on Bradley. Something has to happen to him."

"At least he think he knows what he don't want. Some of us don't even know that. But we have a lotta time, eh?"

"Don' matter how much time you tell yourself you have, things have a way of making themselves felt and catching up with you. And everytime things happen and pass on, you tell yourself you missed a chance. Until one day you're old and grey and you wonder what the hell's been going on all around you all your life. Look at all the talking the two of us do, and yet haven't done. But never mind. Take care, and see you around."

He squeezed her arm, smiled, and got into the taxi. They waved to each other until the taxi turned the corner and was lost in the traffic.

"Bradley came in just now, and walked off the job in style," Lewis told her when she returned to her desk. "You miss all the excitement. He and the editor were cussing each other upside down in here just now. They nearly came to blows. Bradley said to tell you he's going to the interior, and he gave me this to give you." He handed her a slip of paper with a female name and a Charlestown address in Bradley's handwriting. "He said to tell you to post the thing you promised him to this address. He said the person concerned expecting it."

"When things happen, they happen all at once," she said.

"This was happening a long time ago," Lewis said. "Bradley was always threatening to go and live in the interior and looking for an excuse to cuss the editor and walk out. Now Paul gone. Stamp going to the States soon too you know - he's going to study journalism. I won' be surprised if he leaves before that, as Bradley and Paul not here now. I don't think he would be able with the pressure the editor will turn on now. I don't think I will be able either. The rival newspaper been offering me a job long time now, and I think I'll have to take it now. United we stand, and divided we fall as they say."

"I been applying for other jobs," she said, "and for a place at the university."

"You been here only a short while," he said.

"It seem longer," she said, "like a whole eternity."

"Don't let the things that go on here be the measure of eternity. Eternity made up of better things," he said.

That afternoon, she cycled home with Lewis. He said he was going to show her eternity on a canvass, and explained that he painted.

Lewis lived with his family in a flat in Kingston. The sitting room was clustered with chairs - four morris chairs, two Berbice chairs and two settees. A narrow passageway led to the bedrooms and the kitchen. His paintings hung on the walls of the flat. He told her to look at them while he made some tea.

"What you think of them?" he asked when he returned with two cups of tea.

"I like them," she said. "They're very beautiful."

He smiled. "That's all?" He was pleased but could not bring himself to show it, not to a woman.

"What else you want me to say? I don't write the reviews. You do. I never knew you painted. Why you never exhibited?"

He shrugged. "Why should I? I didn't think people would like them. No drama. They're too personal."

"Is that a crime? Who says the personal has no drama? Do you believe that? I don' think you would have painted them if you did."

"I showed them to Bradley, and he said nothing."

"You want Bradley's approval before you can believe in your painting?"

His family were arriving one by one. His mother was a teacher. She was pretty - Lewis resembled her. She smiled when Lewis introduced them. Her eyes wrinkled at the corners when she smiled. Her face was lightly made up: pale lipstick, vague green eye shadow. Like Lewis when she first met him, his mother was reserved. His father was also polite. He shook her hand, and joined his wife in the kitchen. Lewis's younger brother, Trevor, was in the second form at Queen's College, and

134

his younger sister, Paula, was in the fifth form at one of the girls' high schools. The family stayed in the kitchen while she was there. She heard the noises of their movements and their relaxed conversation. It reminded her of home in Pheasant. Jay and William would also be coming in from school now. They would have early dinner perhaps, in the wooden kitchen warm with the afternoon sunlight slanting through the open doors and windows. Laila would be taking clothes off the line now, and she would linger in the shop before leaving for home, talking with the customers. But this was a Georgetown home, very different.

"I painted that three years ago," he said, pointing to a the painting on the wall behind her. It was a landscape, of a frangipani tree against a background of pale blue, papery sky. "And I painted that one last month." He pointed to another in the corner of the wall behind him. It was a painting of a dilapidated house. He waited while she looked at them. "You see any changes?"

"No."

He looked pained.

"Lewis, your paintings are about the things you see. Why are you worried about what people say about them?"

He frowned. "I don' know. Maybe I will stop painting."

"That would be a pity. Why?"

"I not sure. What you think of painting?"

"I don' paint."

"Never mind. Sit, enjoy the cakes."

They sat and ate and drank wordlessly. He was wrapped up in his thoughts. He sat there over-eating and gulping down one cup of tea after another, swallowing his anxiety in large gulps. He cared too much what people thought about him. He was desperately over-sensitive, made that way because he was so unappreciated. It was easy to sit outside of him and judge him, but only he knew what he felt. People would think him strange, self-absorbed, and he was, but it was not because he did not care about others, it was because he was battling so desperately with himself. His sincerity was always evident. Like Bradley and

135

Paul, he was an open book. Perhaps they all were. Perhaps they needed to learn to close themselves. And then, what would they become? Perhaps not themselves anymore, but part of the amorphous mass of survivors, learning to snap and snarl and keep people away. Now he was chewing away at his underlip. He, more than anyone she knew, struggled to maintain his composure, his dignity. It made him stiff and awkward, and small nervous gestures gave him away. He held his head up, but his shoulders often sagged. The moral struggles within him were fierce. He often lost them, failed to defend women when he should, failed to be the real individual he wanted to be, suffered from cowardice with Bradley, Stamp and other men. He struggled to find values, and honour which did not exist in Georgetown. He felt and admitted his failures more than any one of them, too much, and for this reason she felt compassion for him. Only out of compassion could bridges grow between them, bridges of affection across racial and social difference. Compassion without pity and sentiment. Paul, more than anyone she knew possessed this naturally it seemed, and Lewis fought an inward struggle to possess it. These struggles were clouded now in their youth by their helplessness and the failings of male arrogance and their society. Bradley and Stamp did not have the confused yet saving intellectual ambition or pretensions of Paul and Lewis. Bradley and Stamp made an art of envy and hung any ideas they picked up on that - like Bradley's reading of *Memoirs of a Dutiful Daughter*. Bradley despised women but publicised his reading of the book, turned it into a weapon against women. A little bit of this rubbed off onto the other men occasionally, unpredictably. Lewis had asked her to his house, she, a female, for tea and conversation. He liked to act the gentleman in the group. But now, as conversation foundered, he looked unsure. Whenever he was unsure of himself, whenever any of them were unsure of their individuality, their courage to be individuals, they dropped the attempt, and assumed the group identity, their common protection.

"Your parents nag you?" she asked.

He started, and frowned fiercely. "No. Well, yes, they used

to. When I left school. They wanted me to go to U.W.I. in Jamaica. I din' want to go."

She sighed. "Why do families quarrel over education?"

"It was no quarrel on my part. I jus' didn't want to go. You shouldn't assume it is a problem for me."

"Sorry," she said, taking a cake, amused by his fierce but baffled pride.

"Everyone has a way out of something if he or she really wants it. It's all in the mind," he said.

She thought awhile, then shook her head. "It's easy to say that. Anyway, I can take a change in the subject," she said.

"Why?" he asked.

"Because I don't feel the same way," she said.

He sat back, holding his empty cup with both hands, the cup resting on his stomach. He frowned deeply, bit his underlip, and then stared at the floor between them.

"I better go now," she said, rising.

He followed her to the gate. "You from Berbice, right?" he asked.

"Yes," she said.

"I went up there once," he said.

"You liked it?" she asked.

"No," he said, "not my style. I'm a Georgetown boy."

"People different there," she said, exasperated by the narrowness he was showing now, perhaps to assert his superiority.

He made a cynical face. "People the same everywhere me dear," he said.

"I don't agree. People closer to the past in Pheasant you know. You all don't have a sense of the past in Georgetown."

"I not interested in the past," he said flatly. "If that fascinates you so much, you should study history."

"You damn Georgetown people so callow. I'm not trying to prove anything you know. And yes, I will study history."

His mouth tightened, and he threw away the cigarette he was smoking into the grass. He sucked his teeth. "Life is the same. It never changes. It only takes different forms. We are the same."

"End of conversation," she said.

"All these damn illusions," he said. "The possibilities in all of us the same, timeless. Situations just draw out some things, and play some down. Humanity is boring - the same old repeat over and over - sweaty and exhausting. All our so called differences aren't important."

"What's the point of saying that?"

"So you keep a grip on yourself. So you don't fool yourself."

"And what that produces?"

"You can't go wrong," he said.

"Life doesn't seem to be like that," she said. "It isn't true. You risk not understanding people. It leads to too many mistakes."

"You too sentimental about people. I can't afford that. Too many people prey on sentiment."

"I never felt less sentimental in my life. But I hope I never become as unsentimental as you. I don't think you mean what you saying. I think you being defensive. That can lead to conflict too. Look at the editor and Bradley. Sometimes the violence between them make me think they would kill each other if they could."

"Conflict is the only thing that can exist between those two."

"The editor doesn't bother you?"

"No not really. I know what he is. I think you know what he is too, and what you are. We all know. Why get angry?"

"Don't you feel angry when he insults people?"

"Why should I? People been insulting each other since time immemorial."

"And I was thinking how sensitive you are!"

"I not able with emotion," he said flatly.

At the office, she and Lewis shared all the assignments. Lewis worked hard. He blunted himself to the editor, and blind-

138

ed himself to the censorship, the injustices and the indignities around him. He was like a man sitting on a bomb. Ben might have become like him if he had lived in Georgetown, she thought. They both had a great capacity for bottling up their feelings, but Pheasant drew Ben out of himself. He had his village and his people, the things he loved and embraced wholeheartedly. Lewis needed something like that. Perhaps his girlfriend, Mary, gave him that, a private relationship rather than a community.

But Lewis helped her survive. She learnt from him how to bury herself in work, and ignore the minor disasters and explosions around her. She knew within herself that she was living on a surface which she helped fabricate, helping to produce a set mould of easy repetitive communication.

Helen wrote to ask why she never came home. The shop was doing badly. There were frequent strikes on the estate. People were badly off. All the stock had been given on credit. Could Sandra give them a loan, in addition to the normal amount she sent each month. They needed the extra money to stock the shop. Helen apologised for having to ask for the loan. Ben's arthritis was giving him problems. He had to rest a great deal. She could not afford to pay Laila, and was doing the housework as well as baking and minding the shop. She was taking in sewing - all to try and make ends meet.

Helen said she hoped Sandra didn't mind her telling her, 'in passing', that Daphne had written to say that they were not on good terms. Daphne was not easy to live with, but it was important to remember that Daphne had feelings; it was important to try and get on with Daphne, in spite of their differences.

Sandra replied quickly. She apologised for not coming home. Her job kept her busy; she often worked on weekends. She was waiting for her two weeks holiday, and would try to come home then. She was sorry to hear things were so bad, and would send all the money she could. She told Helen she was thinking of going to the university. Perhaps the whole family might think of

139

coming to live in Georgetown; perhaps they could see themselves selling up and trying to make a living in the city. She was sorry that Daphne had written, but there was no need for Helen to fret. It was difficult with Daphne. She was a domineering woman, and the only way not to have a conflict with Daphne was to let her get away with bullying. Helen should not worry about such things. Her own problems were enough.

Son Young and Winston Harris called on her one afternoon. "Remember us?" Harris asked, when she opened the door to their knock. "We were passing by, and thought we would pay a visit."

Young wore sunglasses. He sat in Daphne's rocking chair. "Nice old cottage," he said. "I like it. Nice and cosy."

"Yes," Harris agreed. "Still have a few about. I know this house well. I used to pass it on my way to school, every day, since I was a boy. The lady still lives alone here?"

"Yes," she replied.

"A relative?" Harris asked.

"Yes," she replied.

"The house used to be locked up a lot," Young said. "Remember, Winston?"

"Yes," Harris replied.

"It would still be locked up if I wasn't living here," she said.

"You both teach at the same school?" she asked.

"I teach at a high school," Harris said. "Son teaches at the primary school in Campbellville."

"This lady you're living with - she's strict?" Young asked.

"Strict? How you mean?"

"Restrictive. You know how it is. She minds you going out?"

"What makes you think she minds?" she asked.

"Wouldn't she have pretty tight morals? I mean, if my mother were alive, she would be about her age now, and if she

140

had a daughter your age, she wouldn't let her out of her sight. That's the only reason I asked." he paused, and looked at Harris, but Harris pretended not to have heard. "Look, why I ask is I'm here to invite you to my party tonight. I was trying to lead up to it." Harris laughed low, embarrassed. "I live in Queenstown. The party's at my flat. It's small - only a few people."

"No thanks," she said, "I can't make it."

"If you want to think about it," Young said, "I could call back later."

After Young and Harris left, she sat at the dining table and wrote two applications for jobs, one to the Ministry of Education, and one to a local bookshop. Then she thought about going to bed, but knowing she could not go to sleep she sat in Daphne's rocking chair, rocking slowly back and forth, listening to the street sounds and looking at the night sky through the open window. She was forcing herself not to worry about Ben and Helen. A knock sounded on the door. She looked out of the window. It was Son Young.

"Hi," he said.

"You know the time?" she asked.

He spread out his arms in a gesture of helplessness. "Look, I been kicking myself ever since I left you this afternoon." He waited for her to respond, but she said nothing. "I don't blame you if you think I'm a creep. I got to tell you tonight that I'm sorry."

"You feeling guilty?" she asked.

"I guess that's part of it," he said, "but mad at myself more."

"It's alright," she said.

"Good night then," he said.

"Good night," she replied.

He waved from the street, then was gone.

Son Young continued to telephone. Each time, it was on her lips to tell him she was waiting in Georgetown only to return to Berbice - looking forward to it with her whole being. She continued to refuse his invitations.

He turned up one afternoon, and stood in the doorway, displaying two bags of empty jam jars.

"You have to come and help me," he said. "I'm going to the seashore to collect specimens for a biology lesson. I'm riding a motorbike, and if somebody doesn't hold these bags, these jars bound to break. Think of the children. No specimens for the lessons tomorrow."

She sat on the wall while he searched the seashore. They'd passed through several East Coast villages. A group of boys were swimming in the waves. When he'd filled the jars, he packed them into the bags, left them with her, and waded knee-deep into the water to wash his hands and feet.

The sky was a wall beyond and before her. It was weightless and light blue. Everything was weightless: the swimmers were bobbing in the waves. Further away, near the horizon, the buoys bobbed in the stillness out there. Son was wearing a dark blue T-shirt and blue jeans rolled up to his knees. When he bent over to wash his hands, his wide shoulders and long arms, his trunk and legs seemed, for a moment, precariously rooted to the waves. When he straightened and began walking towards her, he clapped his hands in a gesture signifying that he had finished.

"You won't come out tonight?" he asked her.

The boys were running on the beach now. The breeze pasted their shirts to their bodies. Their laughter was silvery, like sounds from another world, carried by the strong breeze. They ran towards them where they sat on the seawall, jumped the wall and ran along the path leading to the East Coast public road. She counted twelve of them.

"I can't wait to get back home," she said.

He smiled. He had washed his face. His hair, thin moustache and thin beard were wet. He offered her his hand as they climbed down the wall. He held onto her hand as they walked down the path. Dusk was falling. They rode slowly back to Georgetown. The traffic going in the opposite direction, taking people back to the country, was straggly but steady. As soon as they turned into the path leading to the roundabout which straightened into Middleton Street, the strong East Coast breeze dropped behind them, and the warm, damp, familiar city air closed in on them again.

Daphne was descending the front steps when they stopped at the gate. Sandra introduced her to Son.

"I know you," Daphne said. "You teach at the primary school in Campbellville. I have a friend has a son going there. Sometimes I'm with her when she drops him to school, and he point you out to us once. Chapman is the boy's name - Sean. You teach him?"

"Yes," he replied, "I teach him."

They watched Daphne get in her car and drive off. Son shook his head.

"I should be used to it," he said, "but it still gives me a funny feeling when people I don't know say out of the blue that they know me. This place is so small. I wish no one knew me."

"She wasn't meaning anything," she said, as they walked up the front steps.

"That's just it," he said. "It's so normal. I'm not complaining. It's natural. It's just a burden sometimes. It just reminds you how small the place is - even the possibilities of relationships so small."

"You mean people are narrow minded?" she said, opening the door.

"That's one way of putting it." He too, like the other men, could not let her have the last word.

"You'd like some tea?" she asked.

"Thanks," he said, sitting at the dining table.

"What you mean by 'possibilities of relationships'?" she asked him from the kitchen.

She heard him chuckle. "I'm sitting here asking myself just that now." He paused. "I have some friends who been to university abroad. You know anyone like that?"

"No," she replied, bringing two cups of tea to the table.

"They always come back fresh and full of ideas," he said,

"but give them a couple of months, or a year or two, and they come to a grinding halt. They start to talk about being fed up, and disillusioned, and they either go away again, or they stay here and become cynical, or go static in some way. But perhaps they don't go static. But that sort of thing has an effect - makes the place seem small and restrictive. When you're young you don't notice it."

"You still haven't told me what you mean by 'possibilities of relationships'? Do you mean it's too small a world here to have privacy?"

He nodded. "Yes, especially between a man and woman."

"You think that's the problem? Privacy?"

He smiled. "You have a different theory?"

"Life has no centre in Georgetown, so how can men and women have a centre to their relationships? Men lose out a lot in this society but they take it out a lot on women. It's easy, too easy, to treat a woman how you like and get away with it. It's a very macho place, Georgetown."

"And Pheasant?"

"You are accountable to the community. And no, there's no privacy, but you don't need it. Women stick together there too. You will never see women, not in Pheasant, taking a man's side against another woman if he is in the wrong. It worries me how you can be so anonymous in Georgetown."

"You feel anonymous?" He was incredulous.

"Oh yes, and I think other people do too - the poor people. Not people like you, not the families who send their children to the four elite schools. Those four schools are a kind of community, a powerful one, but an exclusive and isolated one."

"So the women are strong in Pheasant?"

She laughed a little, at her own expense. "Too strong. To the extent I feel they are even unfair on men. I've found the reverse in Georgetown. You were talking about feeling static in Georgetown. You feel static?"

"No," he replied, "not really. Not when I'm teaching, not when I'm playing with the band - I play with a small group. I do

144

some sculpting. Not when I'm sculpting. And as long as I'm living alone I guess. I live alone you know."

"You, Paul, Lewis, Bradley - why you all seem the same?"

"You said it, the schools we went to."

"Yet you don't get on with each other. You remember the row at Paul Morgan's party? That was only an expression of a conflict that's always an underbelly of life here - like a nasty current under the surface."

"Yes. I'm used to that. I've seen that sort of row before. Bradley just jealous. He has a hang-up. He has a reputation for being a troublesome fellow. The same people he like to criticize, he like to hang around. Give him a chance to have what those people he criticizes have, and he'd jump at it, and drop all his fighting up and criticism. Human nature is queer. Don't be in a hurry to believe people who like to tell you they have altruistic motives."

"You sound like Lewis. You know Lewis?"

"Yes. How do you mean I sound like Lewis?"

"He says he can't stand human nature, says its boring. He wants to be an individual in Georgetown. But I think he finds it very hard to be an individual here. He distrusts everyone. Everyone tries to believe their own values to be the right ones. For some, material things come first and the things that go with it, for some it's just the right to live their own lives as they define it. They all think their definitions exclusive to their lives. It boils down to one thing - a nagging discontent and insecurity at the bottom of all our lives. It bad enough without us mauling each other. We break the ground under each other's feet, as if it not the same ground we all standing on."

He shook his head. "You're taking the whole thing too seriously."

"Why this constant tearing down of each other? People must reconcile themselves to each other. There's too much rancour, bitterness and cynicism that is justified and normalised constantly, because we can't understand each other. People in Pheasant can recognise greed, vanity and jealousy when they see

145

it, and are not afraid to call them by those names. They don't let it pass. And because they can recognise it, they handle it better. And they don't lock themselves in rooms, or in the separateness of their individuality. They grind away under an unjust system just like people in Georgetown, but they share their emotions, their fears, and their understanding. They not afraid of doing that. That is how they are creative. They scrape some dignity together through a basic regard for each other, by not degrading each other. I not saying it's perfect, or everyone like that, but it is the general standard of behaviour. I think it would seem a lot of naivety and foolishness to city people."

He sighed. "You don't have to live in Georgetown, that's why you can talk like that about it. You just run back to Pheasant when you want to. People here don' have nowhere else to go."

"Daphne said the same thing about my father and Pheasant - that he ran away from Georgetown. But it's not true. Life is harder in Pheasant but people have their dignity."

"I can see you are a difficult lady to please."

"Why women have to be things to please, by which you mean, I think, appease..."

"Dammit man! I wasn't setting out to be superior..."

"But you are. We can't talk as individuals - like everyone else. So you trivialise my views by telling me I'm a 'difficult lady'."

He responded good humouredly, and chuckled at himself, but he avoided her eyes, showing shyness for the first time. She waited for him to become defensive, then aggressive, to refuse to accept the last word of a woman, but he simply sat with her quietly, deep in thought, tracing a slow pattern on the surface of the table. In the silence, the words which had passed between them were easily forgotten; it was so calm between them, so easily had their emotions come to rest mutually. He did not want to contest a position with her. There had been nothing between them before this, no bond of place or race or class or school. That he was a man unafraid of a woman - this was stronger ground for trust. He did not depend on male group identity. His being was not in opposition.

He stood, drew her to her feet and held her near him. He kissed her in the darkening house. He was less sophisticated than David, but much gentler. He was not afraid of being gentle, and it gave him a quiet confidence. Daphne and David were fond of assertiveness, but they had great difficulty achieving it. They resorted to bullying and privilege to assert themselves. She met his embrace gladly, wanting to be taken into his open, direct tenderness.

They saw the streetlight come on like a bright yellow eye near the top ridge of the frame of the window.

She heard him close the front door, heard him start the motorcycle, and heard the motorcycle disappear down the street into the sounds of the city. The streetlight chorused the sky, announced to her that the same sky was cast like thin blue paper over Pheasant, over Helen's and Ben's struggle to preserve the shop and their health. They would be weary now, preparing for sleep.

She dreamt she was asleep in Sarah's room, that the branches of the trees were pressed up against the walls of the room, that Jay and William were asleep in their room, that, in the morning, she would wake before dawn and sit at the front windows looking out at the naked, shifting landscape.

The next morning, Saturday, Son came just after Daphne had left for work. He stood in the open doorway wearing a black T-shirt and khaki trousers. He was very unlike David. She hadn't really seen him before - only the danger of another David. The look he gave her was questioning and grave. His thin, curly hair, tight to the shape of his head, grew back from his temples and downwards again to the vague sideburns at the sides of his cheeks.

"You want to come in?" she asked.

He shook his head. "No, you come to my place," he said.

His flat was on the bottom floor of a tall, sprawling and aged Dutch house. He told her that the couple who owned it lived in the rest of it. The grass was overgrown in the yard, but the tall white fence had been freshly painted. A bookshelf stuffed with books, two single and one double morris chairs, and pieces of sculpture were the only objects in the sitting room. A lattice wall, reaching almost to the ceiling, separated the sitting room from the kitchen. Most of the sculptures, in dark, unfamiliar, firm wood, were unfinished, but the finished piece her eyes lit on was a long thin drum on supports, carved from driftwood. There was another driftwood piece, grotesque in its unfinished state, of what promised to be a human figure. An old piano stood in the corner of the sitting room.

Just before they had left Daphne's, the postman had handed her a letter at the gate. She had recognised Bradley's handwriting. She opened the letter now, while Son made coffee in the kitchen. A postal order for a hundred dollars was enclosed, and a short note thanking her for the loan and promising to pay the rest of it soon.

"You know Stanley Bradley?" she asked when Son returned to the sitting room. "He's in the interior now, and doing all right it seem, thank God."

"You're so wrapped up with these fellows," he said. "Not good. Do they think about you as much as you seem to think about them?"

She looked from him to the letter in her hand. "I'm not wrapped up with them," she protested, "and I don't think about them much. Why do you have to say that?"

He was sitting near her, in the double morris chair. He took her hand. "Don't engage yourself closely in other people's concerns. It's such a small world as it is. People need space to breathe, as much as they need each other. It can cause a lot of traffic jams, especially if you live in a crowded city that's lonely. Never mind your talk about community. Communities like Pheasant are dying."

"What's all this?" she asked. "You're taking me under your wing?"

148

"You're welcome there," he said, hugging her. "Last night when I came in, I sat down at the piano and played a piece of music, and when I wake up this morning, I was still hearing it. And all the way to you I was still hearing it, so its yours. You want to hear it?"

"Yes," she said.

He closed the windows, drew the curtains, and sat down to play with his back turned to her. The music drew her into its slowness. When he finished, he came back to sit near her. He drew her close. She rested her head on his shoulder. He stroked her hair.

"Tell me all about you," she said.

He laughed. "I knew that one was coming," he said.

"You didn't expect I would ask?" she asked.

He shrugged. "My parents used to live in this flat, with me and my younger brother, Abel. They died when I finished high school - Queen's College - and left us with all this, and a bit of money. Abel and I stayed on here. Abel left high school two years ago, and he's married now, and has a child. I been teaching ever since I left school. We didn't always live here, moved from flat to flat when I was a boy, but when we came here we stayed. The old people got on well with the couple upstairs. My old man was a civil servant all his life. He used to play that piano a lot, and sing. And he passed on the sculpting to me. He was all right, the old man. Had a good sense of humour, gentle, kind. The Civil Service treat him badly though. He wasn't a fellow to fight up for position, so he got passed over, but he didn't appear to mind - always with his music and his sculpting. The old lady was quiet and homely." He paused waiting for her to say something. "Not a big family. All our family emigrated - in Canada or England or America now. Just me and Abel. So I guess I'm essentially a loner, although I have a lotta friends."

"Loner?" she asked. "You're lonely?"

He shrugged. "I often wonder. I do all right, so I guess I shouldn't wonder. A lot of people like me about the place. So what? But I know people in big families, some happy in them, some as lonely as they would if they were living alone. But I'm not lonely at the moment."

"Not many people are close to their fathers. You were close to yours, I to mine. Stamp, Bradley, Lewis, Paul and, from what they said about them, Dodd and Harris - they all either lack a father or have a very bad relationship or none to speak of with their fathers. You don't seem a loner to me. Don't call yourself a loner. You're more sure of yourself - you shouldn't let it bother you. Don't feel guilty because you're not so insecure as a man."

"You think I'm not?" There was a playful tone in his voice.

"I hope you're not. I felt you were not. You think you are?"

He sighed. "That's a difficult question."

"You went to school with Dodd and Harris - Queen's College?"

"Yes. A very class conscious, very arrogant school."

"It affected you?"

"Must have done."

"How?"

"I'm not sure."

"Open the windows now," she said.

"No," he said, "I want to get used to you and me." She laughed. "You should laugh like that more often," he said. "Life isn't all about thinking about what other people say and do, you know. Don't get me wrong - I'm not saying that's not important. But you can tie yourself up in knots with just that. This is a big country if you want it to be, and there's a whole continent behind us, and all the islands, and more continents in the world. You see that motorbike? I do a lot of travelling on it. You want to come with me?"

She laughed again. "That's a lot of travelling, and a lot of time."

"We have time," he said, "as much as we want to have. When you talk, you frighten me in a way - as if you think it's the last few minutes left in your life to say what you want to say. But you tell me how little time we have, and I'll show you how much time we have."

She placed his palm on her cheek. "You're right," she said, "but if you'd told me that before I came to Georgetown, and just after I leave school, I wouldn't have believed you."

Every afternoon, they rode out to the East Coast, stopping each time at a different shore - as far as Mahaica -looking for curious shells on the beaches, driftwood, claypipes and stones and specimens that might interest his children. Sometimes they stopped at the homes of his pupils, and were feted with coconut water, rum, mutton curry and cook-up. Weekends they rode along the McKenzie highway, stopping to climb mountains of sand, descend the ridges leading to a cool creek or stream, and shelter in the trees. Their walks became an unending ritual, as unending as the time they spent together in the flat. The routine of her work, the heat and hurry of Georgetown, Daphne's wordless disapproval, were stones that dropped soundlessly into the ocean of her peace with Son.

Helen wrote to say that Daphne had written to 'inform' her that she was going out regularly with 'a teacher fellow'. Helen said she hoped she knew what she was doing. She showed the letter to Son.

"Come and live with me," he said, when he finished reading it.

They were sitting in Daphne's cottage, having just left work. She remembered what Pat had said, and chuckled.

"I not joking you know," he said, serious.

"If I thought you were, I wouldn't answer you," she said. "Once I told a friend of mine that we should get a flat together, and she said her mother would die. What of us two?"

"I not your friend. This is different," he said.

"Very different," she said. "You realise how different? My parents so used to my ways, they would have understood where my friend was concerned, but where you're concerned, it would kill them - metaphorically speaking."

"I'm thinking about us," he said. He paused. "You understand that?"

"Yes. I told her that it seems everything a person wants, something you don't want goes with it. You're not tied up closely with anyone, or else you would understand."

"I'm tied up closely with you," he said. "We want to find out how close or not? You don't understand this doesn't have anything to do with the whole blasted population?"

"I going back to Pheasant soon anyway," she said.

He said nothing, only leaned back in his chair, sighed, and closed his eyes.

"Why you're smiling?" he asked.

"I was remembering Daphne," she said.

"You ever stop remembering people?" he asked cynically.

"She would want to know what *nation* you are."

"And what would you tell her?"

"That I didn't know, because you didn't tell me."

She moved closer to him, and he hugged her. He shrugged. "My maternal grandfather was Hindu, his wife was Chinese. My paternal grandfather was Dutch and African and his wife was Amerindian. It didn't use to be an issue what race you are except when it was a jibe and it hurt, and then your mother and father, if you lucky to have one, would soothe it like so with a kiss. Later it makes your blood run cold - when somebody look at you funny and ask you what *nation* you are, as a condition to something. I used to be called 'Buck' at school. It make you wonder what the blasted hell it is to them. And you soon find out that it to reduce you to a little fish in the ocean - to dispense with you with one greedy gulp. Look at that on a mass scale. What whole races and people get overrun for."

Sandra asked, "Why did it hurt when they called you a Buck?"

He sighed. "I'm not sure." Then he changed his mind. "I think it made me feel confused, not sure who I was."

"You know I'm mixed race too," Sandra said. "My mother is part-Indian, part Chinese, my father is Chinese."

"Does being mixed race make you feel confused?"

"Not being mixed race, no, that doesn't bother me. Not yet. But I wonder if one day it will. In Pheasant my race didn't seem to matter to anyone. Not until I went to school in New Amsterdam did it matter. In New Amsterdam and especially here in Georgetown, Indianness, as I lived it in Pheasant, is alien and I can't be that part of myself here. Here in Georgetown I'm not treated as a rural Indian. I think I'm seen partly as Chinese, but mostly as someone on my own, as an individual. At the moment I like being the two - feeling a part of me, the Indian part, can be alive in Pheasant, the individual alive in Georgetown."

"Georgetown doesn't make me feel free as an individual. It doesn't make me feel any racial part of me is free either. Colour is important here and status - money and education. The only culture that matters now-a-days is American culture."

"Race is the worst problem in Guiana. It's a xenophobic country, maybe because we have so many races and we don't have a philosophy to accomodate all of us."

"This country has no philosophy. Just conflict. You can't liberate one race by keeping down another, only corrupt them."

She held his hand. "You know before I left Pheasant, I was aware how much rural people feared Georgetown and I can see things here to fear. People live as if they have no past and no future. Yes, skin colour matters in Georgetown, not in Pheasant. Class differences are very strong here. Bradley was always trying to fit me somewhere into Georgetown's conflicts. The first thing he asked me was whether I went to Bishop's. He couldn't understand I was from the country. None of them, except Paul, understood. They kept seeing me as a Georgetown person, a middle class Bishop's High school female fallen into their working class company, to be gotten at or protected, sometimes both at the same time."

"Working class? Bradley? Stamp? They went to St. Stanislaus, the others, me, Dodd, Harris, Lewis - all Queen's College. Only Paul went to Central High School, a mixed school."

153

"But all of you are not middle class - your family struggled to send you to those schools, just like Paul's. Those schools are there for the professional middle class, and you all were lucky to go there. Going there made you lower middle class, but your parents are not. Though perhaps of you all, Paul is closer to his roots, and more tolerant of women, less ambivalent."

"Look here, you been reading this communist propaganda the last government bring in to this country?"

"T was right, but not exactly."

"Who is T?"

"A farmer in Pheasant. I went to school with him. He warned me not to come to Georgetown. He said men would not respect me, especially if I try to be their equal. T sees Guiana as two countries, rural and urban. He would never believe me if I tell him that Georgetown people see Guiana as two countries too: the high-colour 'fair-skin' middle class and the swarthy or 'dark' working class. Rural doesn't come into it here. I don't feel I come into it at all. I feel an outsider in Georgetown all the time. I will never belong here."

"Ssh. Don' talk like that. You belong here. Where else would you belong?"

She shook her head. "I don' like Georgetown. The snobbery is terrible. Only Georgetown could produce someone like Stamp. He is trying so hard to become a famous writer, but he really wants the middle class to accept him. And he is just a poor boy, they call him a 'red' boy, from Charlestown. He's pulled by his colour and school into thinking he is middle class, but everything else puts him at the lower end, near the slums."

"You can see it like that because you don't come from Georgetown."

"I know. It frightens me not to belong anywhere, which is where thinking like this leaves you."

He said, "Come and live with me and forget what the family will say. They'll live through it."

"You mustn't think I'm something you own," she said.

"Don't be so jumpy," he said. "That's exactly why I'm asking you to come and live with me. So we can find out how we

154

live with each other - stop living with fears about each other. I always tell myself it's better to live alone, for peace's sake. You see so many marriages in disaster, on the rocks." He paused thoughtfully.

"My parents getting old in Pheasant, like the shop, like Pheasant. Soon Jay and William will leave school, and maybe Pheasant too. What's going to happen to the old people? You know I never visited them once since I left? I can't bear the thought of going there and seeing them getting old and sickly, then coming back to Georgetown. I would want to bring them back to Georgetown. My old lady lived for the day when I would leave Pheasant. The old man would never leave it. I think my old lady would like nothing better than to come and live with me in town, but she feels it's her duty to stand by the old man, in deed if not in word. The whole thing makes me feel so impotent. I want to look after them. But they would laugh in my face if I told them so. That's exactly why I never went back. I would get vex and call them names in the end. I shouldn't even think about it -just accept the situation, like you Georgetown people - square my shoulders and say life is so. If I were a man, that's just the sort of problem would make me go impotent."

He laughed, then suddenly he became serious. "Listen to you," he said. "You frighten the skin off a man. Why you take on so? Your old people sound all right to me. You can only do what you can do. You should visit them. Your imagination runs away with you. You should go back. You would see that things not so bad as you imagine."

"If I went back, they would want to know about Georgetown. They'd want me to open my bags and show them what magic I bring from Georgetown."

"And you would tell them there's no magic in Georgetown to show. Simple as that."

"No," she insisted, "not simple. That's what gets me down, how difficult it is."

The next afternoon, Lewis was waiting at Daphne's gate.

"Hello, stranger," he greeted her.

"Long time no see," she said.

"That's because I always see a certain motorcycle parked here," he said, as they were walking up the front steps.

"That's Son Young," she said, when they sat at the table. "You know him?"

"The teacher fellow? Yes. I know his younger brother, Abel. I and Abel used to be in the same form. We moved through school together. Son was in fifth form when we were in second form. The two of them used to live together in a flat in Queenstown. I used to visit there - a lot. Used to play the piano. Abel working with a big shipping firm now, earning big money. Married, and has a child now. I hear he buying big house soon too. Typical sorta middle class. Stupidy fellow - Abel. I in' able with him these days. All he ever think of was making big money and turning big wheel. I used to like him one time - the days we used to take out girls together."

"Well, Son not like that," she said.

"Oh yes? Well, I guess is because their parents die early make Abel turn hustler. God, when I think of them days it make my skin crawl - to remember what perfect, regular Q.C. boys we were."

"So - you don't see Abel at all these days?" she asked.

"Nah," he replied, "hustling in' my speed. When I meet Bradley and hear him talk 'bout these things, I see the light."

"You should see Son. He sculpts. Seeing you paint, you might have something to talk about, you might have something in common."

"I saw some of his work. One or two driftwood things. Driftwood! But I guess is local stuff and people would like it - as local stuff fashionable."

"His drum sculpture is good," she said.

"Drum? Sound exotic. Back to Africa or India or whatever. What next? Back to China? Back to Portugal? We got to start peddling out the trash fast for the art consumers, girl. Herd art I call it."

156

That night, she laughed as she told Son what Lewis had said. He looked at her gravely.

"Lewis sounds like a creep to me," he said.

"Lewis is not a creep. He's just jealous of you."

"And that flatters you?" he asked. "You're enjoying being the cause of jealousy. See how easy vanity is?"

"Lewis couldn't hurt anybody. He don't mean to. He talks to himself - like all of us do at some time."

"He's still a creep to me. He has to have his cake and eat it by the sound of it. He has his girlfriend and he want to have you too. But anyway, I won't tell you how to run your life. We won't lay down rules and regulations for each other."

"Rules and regulations! You know very well that rules and regulations happen anyway with people. When Lewis was talking I felt like throwing that hot pot a' tea on him. I should come and live with you anyway. Daphne would have a fit."

He laughed. "It might make her wake up and live. She never had a boyfriend?"

"She plays cards with the editor."

They were sitting together in the morris chair, at his flat. It was just after eight. Through the half-open windows she could see the street, half-dark, half-light. The light of a bicycle, car or motorcycle folded into the light cast down by the street-lamp, then the street was still and quiet again. Son seemed absorbed in reading a book. The morris chairs were too low for him. His knees stuck up in them, or his legs jutted far forward, almost to the centre of the circular straw mat in the middle of the sitting room. He spoke often of their need to live together. Would it be different? His face was impassive in the light which fell on him from the lamp on the opposite wall. The light made his skin glow. Had what she told him about Lewis upset him?

"How was I to know Lewis would be jealous of you?" she asked. He didn't answer. His face was impassive to the point of seeming calm, serene. "I wouldn't have thought so," she continued. "He didn't seem the type."

He looked at her superciliously. "You can't assume things about people, or believe what they project. People wear masks.

People are a risk all the time."

"You think I'm a risk?" she asked.

His face broke into a smile. "No," he said. "You think I'm a risk? Look how many times I used to ask you out, and you would never come."

"I was thinking you may be at first. But that was because my first experience with a fellow wasn't too good."

"What happen with this fellow?" he asked, not looking at her, but at the open pages of the book.

"He went back to Trinidad," she replied.

"He's coming back?"

"No."

He said nothing for a while, and she was waiting for him to speak.

"You don't want to know anything else about him?" she asked.

He slapped the book shut, got up and went to the kitchen. She followed him. She watched him closing the windows, slamming them shut and bolting them brusquely.

"You're angry?" she asked.

He spoke without turning around. "I thought Abel and Lewis were good friends. I never realised the friendship broke up. Nothing lasts in this place."

He was disturbed about Lewis, so disturbed it locked her out. And only last night he asked her to live with him. Up to now they had shared everything and allowed each other into their most private confidences. Now she feared that he too, his sense of being a man, was tied up with his awareness of the men he had been to school with. Were the jealousies and rivalries between them a bond more powerful than any with a woman could ever be? Would a woman always be second to one of them? They watched over each other's futures jealously, guarded each other's relationships with women, with ideas, anything which really mattered to any of them. Why could he not laugh off Lewis's sexual jealousy, treat it as comic or ironic? Perhaps because it was not sexual jealousy of a straightforward kind, not jealousy over two men wanting one woman. Was it perhaps the

158

jealousy of the group wanting to possess the sexuality of each other? And she had thought him free of the ties of the old colonial boys' school. He called Lewis a creep to discourage her from liking him, but she felt there was no real conviction in his voice. He was more deeply pained that Lewis and Abel were no longer friends. He had not even noticed her mention of David Petrie, he was not interested, so absorbed was he with his anxieties about Lewis: what Lewis might really be feeling towards him, towards Abel. He behaved as if it was she he was guarding but it was clear it was their passionate male bonding that he was guarding and she feared she could become by their making their scapegoat eventually. The truth was so hard, as hard as it was to under stand how they could be so close and yet so divided among themselves, as hard as it was for them to be individuals yet a group. The failures were the price they faced for not being able to face the truth - the secretive preying on each other's lives. This was the predatoriness Ben ascribed to 'Georgetown people'. She wondered whether it was this lack of a centre which led to communal collisions, the reduction of others to scapegoat status. Lewis, Stamp and Bradley were the unsuccessful sons in families which boasted members who had made the leap into the professional middle class. Were they scapegoats in their families? Was this another reason why they clung so fiercely to the strongest bond they had.

When she got in from Son's flat, there was a telegram from Ben. It said only: "Come home. Helen ill."

She had not opened her empty suitcase since unpacking it the first day in Georgetown. Now she folded her clothes and filled the suitcase carefully, thinking how Paul had gone through this ritual, how he had gone to America, half-fearful, half-ebullient.

It was not just clothes you took with you when you went from one place to another, but all the trappings from the life you left. She could not fit Paul into any other picture but the Daily Mail's office, and the idea of him in a large city filled with skyscrapers was unnatural. Because Paul despaired, she could only imagine him despairing about the skyscrapers. She had tried to picture Sarah and Helen in Georgetown, not as one-day visitors enjoying themselves there, but with their natures entangled with its currents.

Switching off the light and getting into bed, her mind was entirely with Helen. She was glad she had come to Georgetown, not for the reason Helen wanted her to come, not for the reason she had given: to get away from Pheasant. She had not liked Helen's reason; it was asking her to get away from Helen herself, from Ben, T, Pat, everyone. It was release from her own rage and frustration Helen wanted, not from a place. Helen had had rage and frustration here, in Georgetown, and she had taken it to Pheasant where it had continued to haunt her. When she went to live in Pheasant, she blamed Pheasant for it, located the cause for it there, and saw release from it in escape back to Georgetown. Helen's rage and frustration were her own. No one else could find a better place for her. All this time she had tried not to judge Helen. Everyone had their mystery, their tangled conscience, it was a question of getting to know them. Helen was driven, like Bradley, Stamp, Dodd, Lewis, driven by the power of Georgetown. Rushing from place to place did not end a rage or frustration. You had to create your own currents in a place and learn to live with a place too. Ben's contentment was a current, his own which he had created in the space of Pheasant. He did not want to live in Georgetown because it was a place where people fought over and were driven by a power that they thought resided there. But it was a symbolic power, a power no-one here in Guiana really owned. In Pheasant, the power of the English managers and overseers was real. It could be challenged, as it continually was by men like himself, Joe Bachan and others, struggling to achieve better living conditions. In Pheasant, their community was separate from the overseers and possessed its own resources; in Georgetown, the people were wholly enmeshed in the culture and values of those who had bequeathed them the symbolic power over which they fought.

160

III

The Torani was an hour late. The long wait had subdued the passengers who were scattered in a queue of cars half a mile long, crowded in the large sheltered area behind a row of hucksters' stalls and pacing the open platform where the view of the river and outlying banks revealed how the water could push the land back to finite proportions. The trees and shrubs on the horizon were stubby fingers of inky-greenness. The sky was a papery blue, shaded by misty wisps of cloud: a vast hourglass-like wall and ceiling.

The black and white hulk of *The Torani*, drifting closer, grew from toy-like proportions until it loomed large at the stelling. The Harbourmaster blew his whistle and called, "Time! Time!"

As she waited at the stelling, Sandra watched the customary routines: the sailors from the lower and upper decks of the Torani and the stelling shouting, abusing, haranguing: man-do-this or man-do-that, or what-the-hell-you think-you-doing: all the confusion necessary to shift the boat into place and secure its ropes to the stelling; the ropes being bound, the mechanical gangplanks shivering into place; people on the lower deck, the hucksters and farmers, eking out first, pushing barrows, carrying crates, sacks and huge baskets; people issuing from the upper deck in thick queues; then queues of trucks and cars being let on in stages, the trucks first, directed by the sailors with more hurling of abuse and commands. Finally, when the boat was loaded, the gangplanks secured, then as now, the Torani crawled across the water once more.

She stood at the rails on the upper deck and watched the boat part the water. It took twenty minutes or more for this powerful boat to cross a mile of waterway. Some years ago, when *The Torani* replaced the small steamboat, *The Pheasant*, the Maths teacher had proposed that *The Torani* could zip across the water in seconds flat if its engines were on at full power, but then, he'd said, it would probably finish up mudbanked on Crab Island.

In her memory, this journey as a child jam-packed thigh-level with the adults on the single deck of the old steamer was a much more livewire thing. There had seemed a roar of noise across the river. Nothing roared now, only her imagination. It was the drama of a once-in-a-life-time, once-in-a-blue-moon trip to Georgetown. As the steamer filled to capacity, it used to lurch, the water-sodden planks creaking when a lorry boarded. It used to shuttle like a slug when it began to inch away from the stelling. Each wave was a slap which pushed it off course. The wind and rain stopped it in its tracks, with its load of people, animals and vehicles. She didn't feel the discomfort of being squashed in a crowd of adults on the old, damp, rickety steamer. She felt she was standing with them on a stage, and they were all involved in the drama of going to Georgetown. Sarah used to stand firm, with a smile on her face, happy to be going to recapture the feeling of her past youth and strength. Infected by Sarah's expectations, she held on to her skirt and buried her face in her hip-bone. The breeze was cold and whip-like, and morning was breaking as it could do only in the middle of a river at four a.m. The light had changed as they crossed the water. When they reached Rosignol, the sun was a ball of light in the sky, casting everyone and everything into teeming moulds of colours and noises.

On the other side, the Harbourmaster was there, wearing his khaki uniform and cork hat. He stood in his doorway, watching the unloaded passengers and vehicles go past. He was the most unimpressionable man on the stelling, always there, always watching with the same dispassionate gaze, bored by the beggars and the rages of the drivers when the steamer couldn't take their vehicles.

There had once been a pier there made of wooden planks; a passing car would set it rattling so much the pedestrians had to stand aside until the rattling subsided. Now the pier was replaced by a road, and it was a slow walk to the bus stop.

The country buses were parked outside the cinema. The little town seemed slower than it had ever been, the gossip in the cake shops more tired: the mayor was a scamp; what he was doing with the citizens' money only God knew; and what happened about the new housing scheme - the contractors took the money and never built it. People from the old days were still about: Mr. George-the-man-with-one-leg, and Mrs. Simpson, the old firebrand who lived near the school and sold fudge and home-made cakes. They never remembered the young who left for the city; they were used to them going away. They were more old, more grey, peering more intensely from behind their spectacles. Only the young people who were too poor to afford to go to school remained. The town was doing badly. Georgetown sucked people and money away; the merchants, lawyers and doctors spoke continually about not being able to afford to live there anymore; teachers stayed long enough to feel keen discontent before they went abroad to change their professions.

She noted that the Ali family still owned the buses. Ali was heavily bearded now, and greying. The aged Sadhu was helped on to the bus by a small boy. He limped badly, clutching his walking stick in one hand and a medicinal bottle with a white label. Years ago he had read her palm and said: "Go North, Beti." Now he didn't recognise her.

Darkness fell during the journey to Pheasant. There was not a soul on the road. Outside the house, the bus revved its engine, then shot off into the night. The lamp-posts were like wands, holding up a finger of light to the unseeing sky. Where she stood at the roadside, she could see the lamp in its place, dangled from the hook from the ceiling. Ben was sitting at the window, waiting up. Jay and William sat with him. There was no sign of Helen.

They came to the landing. Her suitcase and her feet dragged as she climbed the steps. Jay took the suitcase and William harassed her, wanting to know if she had brought him a gift from Georgetown. Ben shooed him away to his room, and they sat down to talk at the table. Jay brought out Sarah's lamp, the shade polished and clean, the wick burning with an even, smooth flame.

Ben was unshaven, his face haggard and drawn, bags under his eyes. He dragged his hands through his uncombed hair. He looked worn-out and exhausted. "I don' know what befall us girl," he began. "I think Helen dying." He avoided her eyes, his own unable to find focus. "The illness and the operation break her. I don' think it just that. The whole estate running down, with the strike, trouble with the union. The manager threatening to close everything down. All that break Helen spirit. All she could talk about is how she waste her life here with me..." His eyes became damp, but he blinked back the tears.

She comforted him, "Don't blame you'self. You not responsible for these things. You don't control the estate or her illness..."

"I feel she right in a way..."

"Hush, don' talk 'bout anything..."

"She in the public hospital. One commotion surround everything. She just drop in the kitchen with pain one day. Mitch and all of us take her to the private hospital first. The docto' there keep her whole night an' charge me a hundred dollars, then tell we nex' morning to take her to the public hospital, that he couldn't do nothing. At the public hospital, the docto' there kick up a fuss, say the private docto' shoulda known to send her there at once. We all feel so shame. He say we country people stupid..."

She stopped him. "Don' talk. Tomorrow I will go see Helen. You go to bed."

He shook his head. "Sleep don' come anymore. I worrying all the time about Helen, if she die..."

"I will go and see her tomorrow."

"You think we should move to Georgetown? Life might be better..."

"Don't think about that. Just go to bed."

He went to his room, muttering to himself. She took Sarah's lamp to her room. It was dusted and clean, the bed made. She lay on the bed. Her thoughts threaded back to the night she left for Georgetown. They were all right then, as if nothing could go wrong. Helen was strong, in good spirits when she left, and Ben was fully occupied in the life of the village. There seemed plenty of work on the estate. The editor's and Stamp's current affairs lead stories proclaimed each day that the country was heading for a bright future with the new government, that the face of the nation was changing for the better, independence was coming soon. If Daphne's cottage and the houses in Bel Air Park were narrow islands of comfort, then this house was a sinking desert of shifting sand, tottering with despondency.

Jay was strumming his guitar. She went to his room. William was asleep on his own bed. Jay sat on his, the guitar across his knees. She sat near him.

"How?" she asked.

He shrugged. "You talk to the old man?"

"Yes."

"He in a bad state. I never thought I would see him break so easy. All his money gone on doctor's bills."

She got up, and went to the bookshelf near his bed. It was crammed with her old schoolbooks. Undusted, each was stiff from disuse. Her childish thoughts sprang vividly to life, unclothed by inhibition, her handwriting jointed and looped in dried, fading ink.

He strummed as he spoke, "Noor, Nurse, Zena, Miss K and Miss Barry come in everyday to do the housework. They all hysterical. You know how it is when trouble hit them. Illness like an earthquake here. They in and out of the house like is a public road..."

"Don' talk like that. It's natural when this happen for people to help out..."

"Is not that annoying me. Is the way they treat me like some shirt-tail boy."

"Don' be angry. Stay calm..."

"But the old lady too. When I go to visit her at the hospital, she not too poorly to dress me down. They all get hung up and strung up. I so fed up, I looking forward to leaving this place. I hope the old man decide to go to Georgetown..."

"How's the old lady?"

"You will get a shock when you see her. She lost weight, and gone senile. She had a hysterectomy, and can' seem to recuperate." He paused. "You want me to come with you to the hospital?"

She went to the door. "No. You go to school."

At dawn, the village lay unperturbed in the soft light. There seemed space enough for every occasion: birth, life, illness and death. Peace lay real and full in the silence. When the sun dried the dew, the breeze would bring the first movement and the light transform every texture. The canefields would glint in the sun, their sheaves like spears in the distance. As long as they slept, their spirits unhaunted by the day's labours, all was calm.

The hospital was a huge, elongated wooden oblong. It filled the length of one side of the street. It marked the end of the bus route. Years ago, it was painted a colonial cream and brown. Now, the paint was fresh green and white.

Outside Helen's room, a group of Pheasant women kept watch. They touched her wordlessly when she approached, their hands, like those of communicants at Mass when they received the host, speaking more eloquently than words.

In the room, Helen lay on the cot on her side, covered by a white sheet. She was asleep. Nurse sat in a chair near her. She rose and gestured that she should be silent, gave her the chair, then tiptoed outside.

Helen was wasted, as Jay said. Her body had lost a third of its size. The life was gone from her hair, with none of the old gloss, the grey streaks like minute veins on a leaf, her flesh fallen like the drying leaf on a full grown plant.

Her familiar objects rested on the bedside table: her brush, comb, mirror, a vase filled with fern from the garden: signs of her old life and energy. She waited, hearing footsteps along the corridor, the nurses' energetic voices, muffled voices from the hospital yard, the distant trundling of traffic. None of this disturbed Helen's sleep.

When Helen stirred, recognition swept her drawn expression. She was weak, and could barely speak. She opened her thin arms, and Sandra leaned over her, to take her trunk and turn her to a sitting position. When she drew back, Helen covered her face with her hands and began to weep. Sandra took her hands away and dried her face with a towel.

"You don't want to waste your energy," Sandra advised.

Helen asked, "Everything all right?"

She nodded. "Yes."

"I worried about Ben and the boys."

"Well don't worry, just get better, and after that, you can worry as much as you like."

"I not going to get better." She touched her abdomen. "I can feel me-self dying slowly..."

"Hush, you don't know that."

Helen nodded. "I know. You know we old women always know when death near. I dream Sarah. She look so happy in the dream. She was never happy here. I di'n make my peace with her when she die..."

"Don't worry with that now. Just think about getting better and come home..."

"I want to die in my own bed."

"You not going to die!"

She touched her arm. "You young, you have a life in front you. What about that young man, David? I thought he was a decent young man. What happened? You didn't get on?"

Her look betrayed her. She ignored the question. "Daphne send her best wishes, and hope you will get better soon."

"Who this teacher fellow Daphne write me about? I hope you know what you doing?"

Sandra sighed. "But all this is the least of your problems."

"Don' waste your life like me."

"Your life not wasted. Ben miss you bad. All your friends too. They thinking and talking about you all the time. They want you back."

Tears filled her eyes. She shook her head. "You don't understand."

"Look, we can argue later. Try and rest. I thinking I have a bad influence on you, encouraging you to talk and talk."

"I not afraid of death, you know."

"Ssh."

"I prayed to God, and ask him to forgive me for my sins. I don' know...." Her voice was failing, her eyelids drooped.

Her physical weakness was making her mind ramble. Sandra saw this, but now, it seemed Helen was right: she was dying. She ran into and along the corridor, into the ward. The cots were crammed close together, and some patients lay on stretchers along the aisle between the two rows of cots. The ward was huge. It seemed an entire village of sickness and affliction, populated by men, women and children, some with a limb in a plaster cast, two men with their heads heavily bandaged, and here and there, bodies lay so wasted and immobile they might be corpses.

A group of nurses stood around a table in the centre of the ward. Afraid of stepping over the patients laid along the aisle, she stood in the doorway and called to the nurses: "Excuse me!"

One nurse detached herself from the group and came forward. The nearer she drew, the more familiar she looked. Then she recognised Madeline from primary school days.

A jubilant smile lit Madeline's face. "Sandra?" she queried.

"Madeline, come quick." She pointed to Helen's room.

They ran together into Helen's room. She had fallen to one side, her eyes shut, her arms limp at her sides. Madeline took Helen's face between her hands, and laid her head on the pillow.

"What happened?" Madeline asked.

She swallowed, her throat dry. "I thought she was dying. I was frightened."

Relieved, she helped Madeline settle Helen's slight, wasted body along the cot; she slept deeply.

"See how your old lady waste away?" Madeline commented, shaking her head ruefully.

"Madeline, you think I could see the doctor? She says she's dying. I want to find out exactly how things stand."

"The doctor is very busy today, up in the operating theatre whole day today. But talk to Matron." Madeline patted her arm.

"Don' fret."

Numb, she sat on the chair, and leaned on the cot, holding her head. "I get such a fright."

"You afraid of death?" Madeline asked.

She met Madeline's gaze. "I must be, to react so."

"You never seen someone die?"

"Yes, my grandmother. But I wasn't afraid then. I was different then, less jumpy."

Madeline said wisely, "Maybe you thought your grandmother time was right. Maybe you don't want your mother to die."

"Why you say that?"

Madeline shrugged. "I see people die all the time. I see how people behave around death."

Madeline looked the same, her skin smooth, with dimples quick to form in the centre of her cheeks when she smiled. She remembered their childish rivalries. She was the last person she would have expected to see in a nurse's uniform, though from her cap to her shoes, the uniform was ill-fitting, too large. Madeline was full of life. Now here she was, working in a hospital filled with human misery and suffering, death a simple business, routine.

The door was pushed open and a tall, imposing woman with a severe face strode into the room. "Nurse," she snapped, "what is happening in here?"

An insolent expression formed on Madeline's face. "Looking after Mrs. Yansen, Matron," she replied.

The Matron snapped, "Are you Mrs. Yansen's daughter?"

"Yes."

"I don't think you should wait. She had a tranquilizer. She will be sleeping a long time. You should go home and come back again later." She turned to Madeline, "Come Nurse, I need you at once."

The Matron's uniform was spotless, without a crease, her white cap, collar, cuffs and apron pure white; a small gold wrist watch circled her slim left wrist."

169

"Matron?" Sandra detained her.

"Yes?"

"My mother: I want to see the doctor, to find out how she is."

The matron shook her head firmly. "Out of the question. Your mother had a hysterectomy operation. She has to be kept here to recuperate. She is receiving all the necessary treatment. All she has to do is co-operate, and she will get well. I have to go. I have a ward to feed." She swung on her heels and strode out.

Madeline sucked her teeth. "That hard so-and-so, she like to throw her weight about. All the patients afraid of her. She like to terrorize everybody. Never mind, I will drop in on the way home and bring news. You better go now."

The centre of the town rang with life. Outside the market, the country buses lined the road. The hire cars, buoyed in the centre of the bustle of people, blared their horns, the drivers bullying for passengers. The sheltered market spilled onto the pavement: porters pushing barrows, female hucksters in soiled aprons, the buses' engines rumbling near the pavement while the country farmers unloaded their crops: a sustained, chaotic chorus of noise.

The town had been a more vital link between Georgetown and the villages than it now was. Coming from the hospital, numbed by shock, it woke echoes which had become silent, each echo a ripple from the source, Pheasant, where her memory was rooted. Boarding the bus, the villages its destination, it was possible to travel across these ripples.

She recalled how every rickety, madly-coloured country bus, merchant's lorry, cyclist, horsecart, draycart and car used to stretch the full limit of their speed on the road outside the school where all routes met and intersected. The two main streets in town, flat strips of road levelling parallel through it, tacked adjacent from the rim of the red path which separated the bauxite village from the town, ribboned into pathways squaring the suburb where the high school was hatched, and, like the wide trunk of a curved arrow, shot off towards the swingbridge and dived into the fishing village where nets stained black by mud hung drying in the yards. The arrowhead was a Medusa's head of tangled curls: the two widest follicles were the two main village roads, both terminating on the edge of rough virgin land where the silence spoke only grassy whispers and the forest by the riverbank leafed its misgivings.

Covered lorries, green tarpaulins flailing in the wind, had churned round the bend near the school. Their engines foamed noise, guttural r's clamping out the French mistress's voice, so fragile even the breeze pierced its honeyed, open-ended cells. The lorries took barrels of pickled meat, crates of salted fish and cheap wares to the villages. Grocers' children, still in school uniforms, helped clear the counters of sacks of sugar, salt, rice, grain, in half-dark, dank wooden shops, putrid with the scent of aniseed, chocolate, garlic. At the roadside, the men's cries had rung round the lorries as they yielded cargo brutally to each man's back: one hundred pound sacks and thunderous barrels of oil rolled up wooden slopes of bridges. The women fingered exotic enamel patterns on cheap tin plates. Rich subsistence thrived in the ecstasy of uncovering the month's wealth of stock.

She pictured the bicycle groups of schoolgirls in royal blue as they potholed over red-dust roads through armies of canecutters, each carrying a stained canvass bag and a pitchfork on his shoulder, some glancing from beneath the rim of their cane-blackened, floppy hats, returning the schoolgirls' gaze. Then the cyclists would break into the smoother road between rows of sunlit bungalows; through ten villages. Approaching the highway, they raced the buses down the slope of the swingbridge and freewheeled, hats flying in the wind. Friends leaned from choked bus windows, clawing gaily at the air. At midday, those who dared the sun, braved it home to hot lunches waiting in a wooden kitchen eased with shade. The quiet of a country house was worth the hard ride home. On the last day of school, the classroom doors were shut finally, the auditorium and playing fields abandoned.

When she got back to the village, she stopped in to see Pat. She was working in the kitchen, her back to the door. On hearing the knock, she turned around. Her face cleared.

"You come home!" Pat exclaimed. "You stay away so long!"

"How're you?"

She spread her arms wide. "Mummy and Daddy divorced. They're living apart, he in town, she here. You went to the hospital?"

"Yes."

"I think you have to brace yourself." She shook her head. "Time is an amazing thing. Who would believe that only two years ago..." She gestured through the house, towards the road. "We were going to school. It take some getting used to, this being out of uniform, eh?"

"I hear there's trouble on the estate."

"Yes, politics being brought down from Georgetown, Daddy said. He thinks the estate could shut down eventually if it goes on like this. How's your job?"

"There's trouble there too. Politics again..."

"You mustn't get involved. Once you become involved in politics, Daddy says, it spoils your life for all time..."

"I don't know, Pat. I think we're involved whether or not we like it. I think there are times when you can't avoid the fact you're involved."

"You'll stay on?"

"I'm thinking 'bout going to the university."

"You making decisions!"

"What about you? Why not apply for a place? We could go together."

A mischievous look came to Pat's face. "You were talking like that before you went." She ran her palm along the ridge of the verandah. "I have something to tell you. It'll answer your question."

Pat's profile was ringed by the bright sunlight. Here in the shade of the verandah, she leaned against its low wall, the sky behind her. The puffs of white cloud were pierced with the

172

sunlight, the air like water in a white enamel basin.

Pat seemed more womanly, though Sandra couldn't decide where the change lay. Was it in the look in the eye acquiring depth, new postures tried out?

When Pat was nervous, she became evasive. She proffered her profile or stroked her arm. Now, she folded her arms and pressed her bare toes along her left foot. She said, "I'm going to get married." She shot her a half-playful, half-haughty look. "Well? Congratulate me!"

"Congratulations! It can't be someone I know."

"No. His name is Sean, Sean Moore. He and Mummy get on well."

"The important thing is you're happy."

"Yes, I'm all right."

"Pat, we're getting older and older."

She laughed, and shook her head. "You sound like forty, the way you talk."

"I feel exactly my age."

"What about David Petric? You still see him?"

"No."

"What happened?"

"Never mind."

"What went wrong?"

"Nothing ever really started."

Pat sighed. "Why can't people get on? Why you disagreed?"

"We didn't disagree, just lost interest. I must go."

Under the bridge which separated the compound from the factory, the disused canal was overrun by tall grass, weeds and bush. The razor grasses smelled faintly of green mangoes. Black sage grew freely there, spicing the air with its vague cinnamon scent. The breeze carried the scents of the canefield everywhere. From the factory came the smells of processing which the cane underwent, the fruity, mature cane which, after burning in the fields, was brought along the canals to be broken and squeezed until the juice ran in streams along the aluminium shafts into the vats; heated and boiled, the juice was converted to rich, intoxicating syrup, molasses, brown sugar, the vague perfume of the young cane still lacing their richness. Under the bridge leading into Pheasant, weeds lined the sides of the canal. It brought the dank and salty smell of the river in the forest here, mingling with the scent of the rotted cane which formed beds on the floor of the canal, built up over years.

The band of women were waiting at the house: Nurse, Noor, Miss K, Zena, Miss Barry and her aged mother. "Come girl, come and sit down," Noor greeted her, drawing her into their group, round the kitchen table.

When they wanted to talk, they met here with Helen. Their conversations were almost sacred. They came at nights, with their blankets wrapped round their shoulders, bringing their small kerosene lamps, a candle or torch, drank cups of tea and talked long past midnight. They would shoo her away when, as a child, she wanted to listen, saying they were talking 'big woman story'.

The large greenheart table, handed down by Ben's parents, was battered from use, the surface pale and shiny from repeated scrubbings. Noor rubbed her palms slowly along the surface. "Beti," she said, "you see Helen?" When she nodded in reply, Noor nodded. Her long, thick, greying hair hung loose along her back, trapped by the grey blanket around her shoulders.

In their appearance each differed, but their blankets, each a different colour, faded and worn, gave the group a uniformity. Their solemn faces reflected a uniformity of purpose too.

"Helen need strength," Miss K enjoined.

"Courage," Zena added.

"We have to pray for her," Nurse stated.

"She was always a strong woman," Miss Barry began, drawing breath. "Normally, we accustom to depending on her. She accustom to people depending on her. But now, she has to depend. This is why she not happy."

Nurse said, "I know Helen from the time she come to live here. She bring cheerfulness with her, brightness, liveliness.

174

Was always like this and always will be."

It was a ceremony for invoking Helen's heroism. Anecdote built on anecdote, assertion on assertion, passed from lip to lip, like a chalice or a spell. Helen's spirit was broken. It was their duty to mend it. They met here to stitch and repair their lives, whatever setback, minor or major, afflicted one of their number. Tonight, they were including her.

When Son was sure that he was in Pheasant, he began to search for Sandra's house. She had told him that hers was the tallest house in Pheasant, that the bottom storey was not open since the shop took up the bottom half, that the top-half was encircled by closed windows, the roof cutting the skyline in different shapes, with one side a downturned V-shape and the other sloping at an angle nearly vertical with the horizon: green corrugated zinc topped by the dome of the blue sky paled by straggly, wispy clouds. His eyes, following downward, found a flat, shrub-laden land and deserted open houses.

"The people - men and women - work all day in the factory and canefields..." she had said.

Her voice was a memory and a whisper here. She was here, mysteriously, hidden from sight. The thought was reassuring, clarifying all: the silence, oppressive stillness, the hovering and dusty road. He had walked all the way from New Amsterdam and had felt like a man in a desert, passing all the empty, open houses, seeing only an animal, or man or woman or child occasionally, and sometimes a car or jeep or truck driving past out of the blue, in a cloud of dust.

He walked along the slope of the roadside, crossed the wooden bridge and reached the short path leading to the shop. He imagined her presence upstairs. The wide wooden doors were only slightly open; he had to turn sideways to enter. The closed wooden windows let in no light, and his eyes, accustomed to the sharp sunlight outside, searched the darkness within. Wooden cupboards, heaped high on the counter near him,

175

formed a shadowy mound. An open door at the far corner, on the other side of the counter, formed a lighter ridge of darkness. In the shadow cast by the cupboards near him, something white moved on the floor: a man in white unfolding from sleep. Son's vision cleared as his eyes grew accustomed to the darkness. The man showed a handsome, whiskered face. He was wearing a tattered schoolboy's cap. He stretched forward a muscular dark brown hand.

"Ah want a cent," the man said.

Unthinking, Son searched his pocket, drew a twenty-five cent piece, and placed it on the man's palm. His fist closed over the coin. The man's eyes had followed Son's movements hungrily. Now, he curled back to sleep. Son saw clearly now the grey rags which had appeared white in the blinding darkness and the sores gone purple on his legs.

The light ridge of darkness behind the counter was spliced by daylight. Someone had opened a window somewhere. A man stepped through the doorway.

"Yes?" he asked Son.

"Is Sandra home?" he asked.

The uncurious, torpid look on the man's face turned to one of profound indifference and, wheeling round, he disappeared through the doorway again.

"Sandra!" Son heard him call sharply.

He heard her coming downstairs, then she was standing in the doorway, as tall as her father. Her image had replaced his, and the resemblance was striking where it might otherwise have been obscure. Her eyes recognised him and seemed to rebuke him with a look of wonder, surprise and questioning. She looked tired. She had pulled her hair back untidily and tied it with a black ribbon at the nape of her neck. She was wearing a faded, unfamiliar dress, her shoulders bare.

"Come upstairs," she said, indicating that he should walk up the front stairs.

She hugged him about his waist after he closed the door behind him. Her hair smelt vaguely of herbs, not of her familiar shampoo, and her body was tense. He put his arms around her

176

shoulders, and rested his cheek on her head. The daylight brightened the room. Ivy grew along the sides and top of the widest wall, opposite the front door. The furniture in the room was worn but polished brightly: four morris chairs, a Berbice chair, a low wide bookshelf filled with paperbacks. The row of front windows to his left looked onto the public road and a path of cottages stretching back to the adjacent canal and horizon of canefields. On his right, the inner staircase led downstairs, from where she had come, and two open windows were clustered with the branches of the mango tree growing close to the house.

She led him to the passageway off the sitting room, and into a small room. The windows in this room were wooden, and were closed, except one which was slightly ajar and let in a slit of sunlight. She stood before the oblong mirror on the wall and untied the ribbon from her hair.

"How you found the house?" she asked, glancing at him, smiling.

"I ask someone," he said.

The light in the room was soft, gentler than the harsh sunlight which had beaten down on him during the long walk, gentler than the sudden darkness of the shop and the brightness of the sitting room.

She was different. Her hair was longer, rougher to touch, the ends split with neglect, and running his fingers under it, it felt heavier. He hugged her to him. Her dress was made of rough cotton and was tight against her as she raised her arms to enfold him.

"You had lunch?" she asked.

"No," he said, but is all right. I not hungry."

He sat in the morris chair opposite her. They smiled wryly at each other.

"How?" she asked.

"All right," he said. "Why you didn't write?"

"I busy bad here," she said. "A lot to do. I got your letter, and was going to write you back. The old lady is in the hospital. Things bad."

"What wrong with her?"

177

"Hysterectomy. She not doing too well. I wonder sometimes if she's going to die, but the doctors and nurses say not." He said nothing. "Well, what you been doing?"

He shrugged. "The usual."

She took the black ribbon from her pocket and began retying it round her hair.

"What you do here all day?" he asked.

She shrugged. "Work," she replied. She sighed. "Just work - like the old lady. In the shop, baking bread, helping the old man with the business. Cooking, cleaning, washing, gardening, going to the hospital every day." She paused, thoughtful. "I start sleeping at the hospital." She shook her head. "That hospital." She rubbed her eyes. "It's hell. It always was there - since I was small. I used to pass it on my bicycle. It's normal on the outside, but go inside and it's something else. After the firs' few times going there, I di'n' think I could stand it, but I get used to it now. I become so familiar, the nurses come to expect me to go and stay all hours looking after the old lady. The suffering in there. Not enough beds for the people. The nurses overworked. Some couldn't give a damn, and those who try get worked to their bones. I don' know how people get better in there. Once, they brought in this lady with a broken back, all the way from up the creek. And they didn't have a bed to put her on, so they put her to lie down on a sheet in the corridor, right outside the old lady room. Everytime I pass in and out that room that day, she was there - thin, thin, short, lying down straight like a stick, her big eyes black and wide open, staring at the ceiling. Whole day she was in the same dirty dress they brought her in with, and the mud was still on her feet, and she had this gold ring in her nose. When I was going home, I saw the woman was lying in her mess - pissed and shit herself, probably out of pure fear, and she was watching me full in my face with her eyes, not saying a word. I cleaned her up and, all the time, the woman just stared at the ceiling and didn't say a word. These poor people from the coun- try - you could see hospital is a humiliation for them. They don't know what to do with themself in there because they not used to being looked after and they not sure whether to expect it or not, broken back and all, and they not sure they living or dying in there. So they either become hysterical with thinking the doctors holding life and death on a platter or they just give up and lie down and wait to die. Now I immune to it too, like some of the nurses and patients, immune to the worst suffering and incompetence you could visit on them."

For a long while, he said nothing, contemplation written into his features as he looked down at the floor. He was far away. He wasn't with her. She was afraid of his presence, yet glad of it. He seemed stricken by his secret thoughts.

"You so quiet," she said. "What happen?"

He got up from his chair and came to sit on the arm of hers. He took her hand. "Look," he said, " is a bad time. Everything happen too fast and at once.   I didn't know your old lady was in a bad way. It would have been better if you'd written me and told me what was happening, so I would know what to expect. I would have told you this by letter and it would have been easier to get used to. But I going away - soon. I never told you anything, but I applied a long time ago for a scholarship to a university in Canada. They didn't write for a long time, so I forgot about it. I don't push these things. You know I teach for a long time and never thought too much about this sort of thing because it can make life so complicated. And just after I meet you they wrote and said no anyway. So I throw that over my shoulder, and was content, was getting used to the idea of just me and you and the teaching. Well, they wrote the other day. A fellow they give the scholarship to turn it down at the last minute, and I was next in line. I had to give a quick answer. Now it fixed up - airline ticket and all. And I going next week. I come right away to tell you, and was hoping you would come back to Georgetown so we could spend some time together, not knowing what the position was here."

She had drawn her hand away while he spoke, and now she was twisting the thin gold ring on the third finger of her right hand round and round.

"Well? Say something," he urged, holding her shoulder.

179

She shrugged. "What to say?"

"Look at you. Why you're so serious?"

"You expect me to laugh?"

"I coming back you know. Three years nothing. I not going looking for Utopia. I know why I going: to do some studying and come straight back home. We'll write, and wait. Eh? Say something and don' make y'u face so long, like is the end of the world."

She turned and looked up at him. Her eyes flickered across his face, and she turned away. He bent forward and kissed her neck, then spoke with his lips near her ear.

"Don' sign off," he said. "Sometimes you so unreasonable. Don't lock me out now. You people behave as if going abroad is the beginning and end of everything. The damn illusion alone is what put me off ever attaching too much importance to going to university. This is nothing to me - just three years of study, then back home to being the same old me. You understand? You don't believe a word I say. Look at you."

He got up, and walked across to the front window.

"Look," she said, "we're not married you know. You don't have to justify anything to me. The fact of the matter is you're going. I'll get used to it later I expect. But I have enough worries with the old people now. The old man is a mess himself."

He walked slowly across the room. When he reached the staircase, he leaned over it and peered downstairs, then swung around, leaned back and folded his arms.

"This place so quiet," he commented. "What you think if I stay here a day or two?"

"No," she said.

"What you're going to do?"

"I can't think of anything else except what's happening with the old man and old lady now."

"You promise to write?"

"I can't promise anything - the way I feel now. I have this one commitment to stay here and help. I can't think of anything else now, truly."

"What time is the last boat?"

"Sometime between six and seven. But you better go now. I have to go and cook something for the old lady now, then the old man and I going to the hospital, and I spending the night with the old lady."

At the door, he spun the loose doorknob and watched it spinning, biting his underlip. "I'll write," he said.

He ran down the front steps three at a time, and left the yard through the side gate. She watched him as he walked along the road. The sun was coming out from behind a mound of clouds, and the spreading sunlight unfolded along the road.

That night, there were two *maticore* ceremonies. One group took to the Eastern half of the village, the other to the Western half. From her window, she watched their progress in the darkness. The lamps in each group traced a semi-circular route, each outer curve extending outward to the boundaries of the village. Her eyes traced a circle by their light. She could imagine the close-up scenes: the crowd of women moving in slow groups, their lamps illuminating their faces. The brass bowls, hung from narrow chains, were swung from side to side as they went. The dusky pink, purple, blue and white smoke, fuming from the bowls, brushing the women's dresses, ethereal, was visible from the window. The groups seemed to move in their own orbit of lamplight and smoke, like apparitions in the dark night. Their drums throbbed, small cymbals clashed, the sounds mixing profusely into the quicker rhythm of the women's chants: stentorian bass voices, caterwauling treble voices, all fusing into a harmonic disorder made purposeful by the ritual, a ritual and noise as intense as that of the powerful predatory birds which carved frantic patterns in the air above the canefields, their shrieks cutting at night into sleep, rousing the senses from indifference, making the heart throb in fear and anticipation. Somewhere, the absent brides, in whose honour the rituals were held, waited hidden from sight, as they would be at the wedding, hidden under layers of veils. At the end of the ritual, the women withdrew to

181

disperse along the paths leading to their cottages - the lamp carrier walking alone, swinging her light, the lone drummer chanting a private quiet song to a private rhythm, to her gate.

Noor came to her room at three a.m. She shook her awake cautiously, sitting on the bed. She held a small kerosene lamp which cast a dull orange light round the room. "Wake up Beti," she urged.

"What time it is?" she asked Noor.

"Two o'clock," Noor replied. "Postmaster just get a telephone message from the hospital. You mus' go quick. Nurse will come with you. Mitch coming. He will drive."

Noor held up the lamp while she dressed. Outside, Zena, Miss K, Miss Barry, Ben and Nurse were sitting round the table.

Nurse said to Ben, "Ben we're not sure what happening. You stay here and, if anything, Mitch will come back and get you. Sandra and me will go see Helen first."

The drive to town was swift. Mitch tensed over the wheel. He yawned deeply once, and rubbed his eyes. Nurse stared ahead, her eyes bright with the reflection from the headlights.

Mitch waited at the hospital gates while they went in. Nurse strode through the darkened wards, stopping to explain her purpose to each nurse on duty there. The cots were bulky with the patients, their bodies, covered by the pale sheets, mounds in the shapeless shadows of the hospital.

Helen was lying on her back on the cot. On the wall over her table the light was switched on. Her hair was combed. Her face looked restful. Her hands lay on the sheet on her stomach, and rose and fell gently with her breathing. Nurse leaned over her, peered into her face, and seemed to search for a meaning not clearly written there.

Madeline appeared in the doorway. "I sent for you. I had the feeling you should come."

Nurse nodded, "Yes, awright. Thank you Madeline."

"I di'n' like how she look..." Madeline continued.

182

"Ssh," Nurse urged. "Don't speculate. You go back to work. We will stay awhile."

Madeline returned to the ward. Nurse drew up two chairs near Helen's cot, sat nearest Helen and held her wrist, feeling her pulse.

Sandra made to speak, but Nurse put a finger to her lips and said, "We must just keep calm and wait."

They sat for twenty minutes or so with Helen, Nurse glancing frequently at her watch, keeping a hold of Helen's wrist, looking anxious. Sometimes footsteps echoed along the corridor, or a patient's groan sounded from the ward.

The first sound came from Helen: a sigh. Nurse leaned closer, alert and relieved. A frown creased Helen's forehead, then the frown disappeared and her face was restful again. But her breathing quickened for a few seconds, then slowed to a drag. She began to inhale deeply, and exhale in sharp, muffled blasts. Then suddenly, she stopped breathing.

Nurse knew at once that life had left Helen. She drew down the sheet, took her hand from Helen's and covered her again. Only seconds filled the gap since her last breath. If time halted, Helen might yet breathe, but her stillness set a seal on it: her life, if it was a life, would clothe their own with substance only their memory could will; her spirit would live on only like the breeze which stirred the spaces between one person and another.

Nurse wept silently, her head bowed, fists balled in her lap, her generosity folded, for once, into her own flesh and converted to her own grief for life. Their silent weeping drew on remorse, like Helen's when she regretted Sarah's passing. Already, they were wedded to her only by communal facts, her voice, will and passions too dead to speak for herself.

In Pheasant, Ben and the women were waiting at the window. The lamp hung like a trapped star in the house, the night like a blanket over the rest of the village.

Ben came to the landing as they mounted the stairs. Before they could speak, he said, "I know, Helen dead."

183

At the funeral, each person, dressed in white, black or mauve, stood at their own height of mourning. Hymns were sung like an offering, passed round the room like a drug on their lips. The coffin rested on a wooden stand. Ben wore his black suit, his face bleak, eyes red. Miss K sat at the foot of the coffin. Her thin, slight figure in her white dress swayed to the tunes, her eyes closed in a dream. She added her own chorus of sorrow or praise to the words of a hymn: "Helen going home!" or "Preserve her spirit, Lord!" Nurse, dressed in black, stood in the corner, weeping silently. Noor stood near Ben, her head covered by a white veil. Laila, T, Estelle, Jay and William sat together on a bench near the inner stairs, T looking older, his forehead lined by a deep, permanent frown.

Pat arrived last, with Mr. and Mrs. Edwards. They stood with her, beside the coffin. Mr. Edwards opened the Bible, raised his hand for the singing to stop, and began to read the twenty-third psalm: "The Lord is my shepherd, I shall not want." When he finished, he turned the pages and read again: "When there were no depths, I was brought forth; when there were no fountains abounding with water. Before the mountains were settled, before the hills was I brought forth. While as yet he had not made the earth, nor the fields, nor the highest part of the dust of the world. When he prepared the heavens, I was there: when he set a compass upon the face of the depths. When he established the cloud above: when he strengthened the fountains of the deep. When he gave to the sea his decree, that the waters should not pass his commandment: when he appointed the foundations of the earth: then I was by him, as one brought up with him: and I was daily his delight, rejoicing always before him: Rejoicing in the habitable part of his earth; and my delights were with the sons of men."

The road was lined by spectators. Mr. Edwards pleaded for a passage for the coffin. Progress to the churchyard was slow. The coffin was precarious in the crowd, on its support of precious shoulders: Ben's, Mr. Shepherd's, T's, Mr. Edwards's, Miss Barry's, Noor's, Nurse's, Mrs. Edwards's.

The Anglican priest received the coffin under the poui tree. The ritual in the church was an interlude before the more intense passage to the grave. There, after more prayers, the coffin was lowered, and the gravediggers began to fill the grave. She watched every shovelful of soil heal the wound in the ground, claiming Helen.

Efforts to rescue Ben from the vacuum into which he plunged himself were fruitless. He went about his chores numb with shock. The women visited every day to warn that, in his own way, he was committing suicide. He cut himself off with silence, as he did when his pride was stung. Helen's disappearance from his life removed the ground from his feet, as did the problems on the estate, shut down now every day, the men restless while the unions and management locked themselves away for talks in Georgetown.

Ben died six months later. She found him when she went to wake him. The closed shop had been impatient for his presence, the men calling up at the windows since five. When she lifted the net and felt his arm, he was still warm. As with Helen, she waited for him to take another breath and, as with her, none came.

They buried him with the same ceremony, by a ritual now clear in her mind. She visited their graves the next day. The villages and factory were hushed. There was no edge to the sun. Noon was yet hours away. Then the heat would be like a compact furnace, parching the land with the sharpest light. The grass was still cool with dew. Wild flowers grew everywhere.

Where she sat, she faced the new schoolhouse, recently built by the estate. The older building, a hundred or so yards away, was unpainted and decrepit. It was decaying slowly, an unintended monument and signal to her memory.

She heard again their voices from the past, the voices of the children she and her friends had been, buried in the echo cham-

185

bers here, as were the noises of their play when they trampled the flowers underfoot, elusive and lithe, vivid as the flowers. They used to hide in the hollow under the church, beneath the altar, talking without fear of adult censorship, their talk plaited with vulgar truths. Above them, on the other side, was the spirit silence of God, religion, worship.

She reflected how Sarah and Helen, unlike Ben, had not chosen when to die. Helen and Daphne had disapproved his laughable poverty. His choices had seemed ridiculous to them because they diverged from the common tracks of men. Everyone in Georgetown and Pheasant laid a claim to the struggle to survive. What did their rage and despair have to do with Ben? He had struggled to survive too, in his own way, unobtrusively, with a naked, neurotic fear and avoidance, like a superstition, of the opportunist in himself. She thought of The Mail, of Paul, Bradley, Stamp and Lewis, of Son's departure for Canada. She knew that she too would leave the village. So what of Ben? Was there no dirge that could mourn his death, no song celebrate the life he had invested in this stranded and exploited village?